The Darkened Mirror

Amanda Crum

An Imprint of Sulis International Press
Los Angeles | London

Library of Congress Control Number: 2019906301
ISBN (print): 978-1-946849-52-6
ISBN (eBook): 978-1-946849-53-3

Published by Riversong Books
An Imprint of Sulis International
Los Angeles | London

www.sulisinternational.com

Contents

*Dedicated with much love
to Grandma Robyn,
whose encouragement
helped me find my voice.*

Part One
Now

Chapter One
Dreams

Josie Burns was dreaming.

She dreamt of a door. It was small, just big enough for her eight-year-old self to crawl through comfortably. She had seen this door before—many times, in fact, during the hours which claimed her mind in sleep-but had never opened it. It seemed to hold secrets too large for its slender frame.

This time was different. She pulled it open hesitantly, its hinges screaming like a wild animal. On the other side, there was only darkness. The sudden hiss of a match being struck alight made her jump, and she turned to find her brother, Andy, squeezing through the doorway. There was something not quite right about him being there with her, but Josie couldn't put her finger on it.

"Where have you been?" she whispered.

"I've been here," he replied. His voice sounded sad. "C'mon, let's go. It's getting late. The Shadow Man will be mad."

Josie jerked awake, the way one does after having a dream of falling a great distance. After a moment of disorientation, she realized she was safe in her bed and let out a ragged breath.

Someone was in the room with her.

She could sense a presence, lurking just outside her peripheral. She lay perfectly still, trying to suss out the faint but unmistakable sounds of someone breathing or the shuffling of feet. After a moment, when all was quiet, she relaxed a bit. *Probably something left from my dream*, she thought tiredly. But her eyes still scanned the darkness of her bedroom, roving over the boxes of her belongings that were stacked in every corner. The face of her alarm clock was blank; the electricity had already been shut off then. Her mother had been tying up loose ends all day, getting things ready for the move.

There was no moonlight to speak of. She could see next to nothing, only shadow upon shadow. Her mind recalled Andy's words in the dream, and she shuddered. Who or what was "The Shadow Man"? In the grip of her fear, she did not recognize the grim reality that should have set in after her brother's appearance in that dream. She did not, after being awoken in the middle of the night, remember that he had gone missing six years ago, when she was eight and he was ten.

Something moved in her closet. Wire hangers clanged together, then suddenly stopped, as though someone had grabbed them. Josie sat up on her elbows in bed, her heart thudding a dull rhythm in her ears.

"Who's in here?" she whispered. The sound of her own voice gave her a boost of confidence: "Emily, if that's you, it's not funny!"

"Josie?" A light knock on her bedroom door. Her sister, Emily.

Josie tried to focus her eyes on the black rectangle that was her closet, but it was no use in the dark. There was nothing to see.

The bedroom door opened and Emily stuck her head in, looking sleepy and disheveled. She carried a small flashlight in one hand, which pierced the darkness in a thin, silvery beam.

"Who are you talking to in here?"

"I guess I was talking in my sleep," Josie said, sitting all the way up in bed. "Bring me that flashlight."

Her little sister did as she was told and then plopped down on the bed, wrapping the quilt around her bare legs. The house was drafty at the best of times, but with no heat, it was downright cold. It was only the first week of October, and already the forecasters were calling for snow, a rarity in Kentucky which Josie dreaded, although she wouldn't be around to see it. Tomorrow they would be almost a thousand miles away in Maine, starting their lives over.

Josie walked toward the closet with slow, deliberate steps, partly in fear of what she would find and partly out of necessity. Her belongings were packed neatly in boxes from the moving company, but there were several of them, too many to really fit in her small bedroom. They were stacked on top of each other haphazardly, some leaning in precarious positions, and if she wasn't careful, she would send them flying.

"What are you doing?" Emily asked with genuine curiosity.

"I just want to make sure I haven't left anything in my closet," Josie said softly, pointing the flashlight straight ahead of her. "We'll be in a hurry in the morning, and I don't want to forget anything."

"It *is* the morning," Emily pointed out with a jaw-cracking yawn. "I'm only up because I had to go to the bathroom. It's freezing in there, by the way. If you have to go, put on some socks."

"Mhmm," Josie said. She was six inches from the closet now, and all was silent. Taking a deep breath, she yanked the door open. It was empty save for several wire hangers, which were moving slowly back and forth as though caught in a slight breeze.

She let out a shaky sigh and closed the door, clicking off the flashlight. Her eyes were better adjusted to the darkness now, and she moved back to her bed, crawling over Emily and snuggling under the blanket.

"Hmph, a nye thin?" Emily mumbled, already half asleep. Josie translated that into "Find anything?" and whispered soothing words to get her sister back into the land of dream. Having found nothing, and with the warmth of the quilt and the comfort of her little sister's presence, Josie felt the tension ease from her body. The noise in the closet had probably been her imagination or just one of the many drafts of air that floated through the old house all the time. She closed her eyes, feeling satisfied enough with that explanation.

In light of the night's events, the dream was all but forgotten.

∞

Josie opened her eyes to find the sun had come up, throwing its weak light over the bare limbs of trees and the dead lawn. Emily, who had always been an early riser, was gone; presumably back to her own room to get dressed for the day. She'd left a warm spot in the bed, though, and Josie rolled over into it, loathe to get up. It was so warm there beneath the heavy quilt and the room was freezing.

Her dream came back to her and she frowned, trying to remember it in detail. There had been a door, she recalled, a tiny door to a tiny cupboard. There had been things inside, but she couldn't quite see them in her mind's eye. And something else, something perplexing...

Andy. Her brother, missing now for six years, had been there with her. She hadn't dreamed of him in a long time. The memory of it made her heartache, and she felt a solid lump form in her throat, the salty kind that always brought tears. It was the sneakiness of grief that made it so terrible, she thought. You could go about your life like always, fill it with school and friends and music, and then one day the thing you thought was gone would roar into full, pulsing vitality. It was always there, sleeping beneath the surface; a great hibernating bear.

Emily came bouncing in, full of pep despite the interruptions in her sleep, and sat on the end of the bed. Josie burrowed further beneath the blanket in protest. At ten years old, her sister was definitely a morning person, and Josie was way on the other end of the spectrum.

"Mom says to get up because the movers will be here in thirty minutes—"

"Ugh."

"—and she said I can keep Ham in the car with me as long as he stays in the carrier."

"Double ugh."

"What did Hamilton ever do to you?"Josie sighed. "He's kept me awake almost every night since you've had him because I can hear him running in his wheel. It squeaks, and it's super annoying."

"He has to run; otherwise he'll get fat and out of shape," Emily replied, rolling her eyes. "Hamsters need lots of exercise. I read about it at school."

"But that's perfect," Josie grinned. "A fat hamster named Ham, how cute is that?"

"You're in a *mood*," Emily said in a perfect imitation of their mother. "How long did it take you to get back to sleep last night?"

"Too long. Do I hear the Bishop Brothers somewhere?"

"Mom let me download their new album! She said it's a moving away gift. She has something for you, too."

That piqued Josie's interest enough to earn a peek from beneath the quilt. "What is it?"

But Emily was already gone, dancing down the hallway back to her room and the Bishop Brothers, whose voices suddenly became unbearably loud through the thin wall.

"Just because I'm awake, that doesn't mean you can blast it as loud as you want!" Josie shouted, banging on the wall above her bed.

"Get over it, turd breath!" Emily called good-naturedly.

"Emily Marie Burns!" their mom shouted up the stairs. "I heard that!" Then, a moment later to Josie, "Get up, kiddo. Time to face the day. If you want your gift, you have to walk downstairs for it."

Josie shuffled from her room. Gift or no gift, the day had several things working against it: cold wooden floors were just the beginning. Several hours from now she would be an official resident of Maine, living in a house with two old women she hadn't seen in years. Everything she knew would be gone or different. Her friends, her school, even this crappy, drafty old house. She would miss it all madly.

"Don't frown so much, you'll get premature wrinkles," Josie's mom said as she trudged into the kitchen. "You want to be the only freshman with crow's feet?"

"Why not? They do it on TV all the time. I'm pretty sure half the people on the Disney Channel are in their thirties."

Her mom smacked her lightly on the bottom. "Well, Miss Grouchy Pants, if this doesn't put a smile on your face, I don't know what will."

Josie looked at the small bundle her mother was holding out and grinned. Beneath a huge red bow was a box of good sketching pens, which Josie had begged for several times over the past few months. She had signed up for an art class at school the previous year thinking it would be easy and, to her surprise, found she was actually quite a good artist. She'd started a sketchbook full of inspirations, but charcoal got messy and sketching pencils required too much maintenance. These pens would be just the thing she needed to complete some of the more detailed drawings she'd started.

"Thanks, Mom! What did I do to deserve this?"

"It's just a little something to show my appreciation for how well you've handled yourself lately. It's been a rough year for everyone." She paused, then went on before Josie could fill in the gap with the obvious. "I know you guys miss your dad. I do, too. I never wanted it to be this way, you know." Her voice took a sad edge, drawing out the last word until it was almost a sigh.

"I know," Josie said. She stared at the package of drawing pens, blinking away tears. She had watched her mother struggle for the past year to keep them afloat, fighting back her own heartache after her husband abruptly left—with no forwarding address—in order to hold herself up for her girls. She hardly ever talked about him and Josie followed by example, pushing back her rage for her mom's sake. They had all seen too much.

Her mom began to busy herself at the counter, wiping away toast crumbs and cleaning the tiles. "Do you remember your aunts much? I know you were pretty young the last time you visited."

"A little," Josie mumbled. "But they're my great aunts, right? Your grandma's sisters?"

"Yes. They're very…eccentric old ladies. I hope you didn't tell Emily any weird stories about them. I don't want her to be scared. She was only four the last time you guys visited and she won't remember."

"I haven't told her anything," Josie said defensively. "I barely remember myself." This was true, although she remembered the day she'd returned home very vividly.

Her mother had already moved on to checking the cabinets, opening and closing them methodically to make sure nothing got left behind. It was her way of showing that she was done talking, a classic

Mom move, but Josie wasn't ready to end it just yet.

"Mom?"

"Hmm?"

Josie paused. She didn't want to cause a fight, not on today of all days, but she couldn't hold it in any longer.

"I had a dream about Andy last night."

All action abruptly ceased in the kitchen, as though time had stopped. She watched her mom's back slump the tiniest bit, and a little worm of worry began to gnaw at her stomach. After a few moments, her mother went back to the cabinets.

"Huh." It was a declaration, as though she had just found an interesting species of bug in the garden.

Josie couldn't see her face, but she knew without a doubt what was there anyway: a tight-lipped almost-frown, the mouth so small and white it all but disappeared. There would be no discussion of her brother, not today. Maybe not ever again. His photos were neatly framed, and they would go up in the new house, Josie was sure; they could remember him, they could think about him, but they did not speak of him. Her mother had given up hope only recently that he was still alive somewhere, and the weight of that hope had been the only thing holding together her marriage.

There were so many things Josie wanted to say, to scream if she had to: *What if we move and he comes back? He won't know where to find us!* and

It's not my fault he's gone! were just a few. But she knew from her mother's posture and the deafening silence in the room that her questions wouldn't be answered today.

She left the kitchen with a heavy heart.

She didn't notice Emily standing behind a stack of boxes in the living room.

Chapter Two
Bedford

The drive from Kentucky to Maine, although pretty, was a long one. There wasn't extra money for airfare, although the aunts probably would have offered to pay for plane tickets had Josie's mother tamped down her pride long enough to ask. It was bad enough she was having to take her daughters to live in a strange town with two elderly roommates, something that made her feel like a failure, which Josie understood only as a vague sense of defensiveness coming off her mother like perfume.

The girls took turns riding shotgun during the trip, switching now and then when they made a pit stop. Josie, being the eldest *(but not really,* her mind whispered, *not if you counted Andy),* wouldn't usually give up her seat, but Emily had been sullen and unusually quiet during the trip. Her sister was always the upbeat, disgustingly cheerful one, and had made past road trips a nightmare for Josie— who liked to put her MP3 player on shuffle and zone out—with her endless knowledge of popular radio songs and the need to play car games, which tore at Josie's patience.

But today Emily simply sat in silence, staring out her window at the passing scenery with Ham's carrier in her lap, and it was so out of character for her that Josie had offered not only the front seat, but her bag of sour gummy worms as well. She planned to corner her sister once they were alone and ask what was going on.

Their mother was unusually quiet during the drive, too, and Josie wondered if she was thinking about her son, how he wouldn't have his room unpacked when they got to the new house. All of his belongings had been boxed up and shoved into the darkest corner of the moving van, and when they arrived in Maine, they would be put into storage. No one had the heart to suggest to Josie's mom that she donate his clothing and old toys. It wasn't something she was ready to do, anyway.

Josie leaned her head against the cool surface of the window and watched as the geography whizzed by, one anonymous town after another. To get her mind off Andy, she turned her thoughts to her aunts.

Joan and Alice were kindly old ladies, she remembered, so at least there was that much. She had only been eight years old the last time they had visited. Until then, there had been sporadic visits to Maine, sometimes at holidays and sometimes during summer vacation, and Josie hadn't known the aunts very well. They were simply two elderly ladies who gave her family a place to stay when they were up north. But the summer she turned eight—the same summer Andy disappeared—her mother had sent the children to Maine to stay with the aunts. Although she hadn't been aware of it at the time, her parents' marriage was in trouble even then, and her mother had seen that summer as an opportunity to set things straight.

Josie and Andy had enjoyed that summer thoroughly, as being without parental supervision was the closest thing to heaven they could think of, and the aunts seemed to understand that having their four-year-old sister under their feet would hamper the fun. They took Emily on day trips to the aquarium and to the library while Andy and Josie slept late and did exactly as they pleased. The aunts weren't strict about bedtimes or treats or anything, really, and had given the children the run of the house. When their parents called to check on them, both sounded happier than they had in a long time, and Josie and her brother sensed that change in mood even though they had both been unaware that there was anything wrong.

But the summer came to an end, and the children had to go home. Neither were particularly looking forward to the new school year and so, after their parents had picked them up at the airport and all the details of their summer adventures had been relayed, the magic of the previous six weeks seemed to fade away. A very curious thing happened to both of them as they trudged upstairs when they got home and unpacked their belongings, although neither spoke of it: their memories of Maine and the aunts and the huge old Victorian house seemed to dissipate with each passing minute, like water swirling down a drain. Josie would recall a particularly fun game she and her brother had played, only to find herself trying to remember what had made her so happy a few moments later. It was odd, and had she been afforded more time with her brother, she would have talked to him about it.

But as fate would have it, she would wake up the very next day to find he had disappeared sometime in the night without a trace.

Her father had taken to sleeping on the couch shortly afterwards.

∞

In the fourteen hours the three of them spent in the car together on the way to Bedford, Emily spoke exactly twice. They stopped at a small motel at dusk to eat and rest before the last leg of the trip which would be finished the next morning, and Emily insisted she was fine both times Josie managed a moment alone with her to ask. Her face remained an impassive mask, which was so unlike the girl that Josie was beginning to feel deeply worried. Emily was the animated one, the one who displayed every emotion she had on her features as though her face were a movie screen. It was Josie who was the stoic one, the sullen teenager who had her reasons for not sharing what was on her mind. Something was going on.

But thoughts of her sister were immediately shoved aside as the car finally wound a slow descent into Bedford, a little burg mostly situated in the cradle between two giant hills. They had traveled on a two-lane road for over an hour before a large wooden sign greeted them: *Welcome to Bedford!* it exclaimed. *Home of the Bedford Bruiser!*

What, exactly, did that mean?

The town itself was one of those New England villages that are usually described as "quaint" and "charming" instead of "tiny" and "boring" which are sometimes more accurate adjectives. Main Street was filled with well-kept storefronts boasting handmade this and homemade that; young mothers rolled their baby carriages between these shops like extras in a film, smartly dressed in pea coats and fashionably knotted scarves which popped in the morning sunlight like brilliant jewels.

In fact, the entire place was like a movie set, as though it had been cut from a film and transplanted into real life. As her mother slowed the car and eased it toward a stoplight, Josie had the unsettling feeling that if she opened the door to any of the shops lining the street, she would find only the other side of a carefully constructed facade, or perhaps a staged set which had no roof and doors that opened onto nothing.

Though she'd been to Bedford before, she realized her memories weren't serving her very well. The town itself looked familiar enough, in the vague way that all small towns do, yet she sensed that there had been changes made since her last visit. She tried hard to come up with a definitive memory of something—anything—on Main Street and was surprised when the only thing that surfaced was the library, an old building with large white columns in front and a clock tower. It had been situated between the County Clerk's Office and a pharmacy, and she had a faint recollection of leaving the blessedly cool confines of the children's reading room with her brother to go next door for a Coke at the pharmacy's fountain.

"I think the house is just up here," Josie's mom said, consulting the directions she'd written down. "Help me look for Wicker Way."

Josie looked over her shoulder at Emily, who was staring silently out the back window at the passing scenery. "Do you recognize anything?"

Emily shrugged. "Not really. I was too little last time I was here to remember much."

She threw a glance at Josie, one so quick it might have been missed if Josie hadn't been studying her sister's face carefully. It was a look that said she *did* remember something, but whatever it was, she wasn't going to talk about it. But more than that, it was a look of fear. Josie turned slowly around in her seat, heart pounding a tribal beat in her chest, and wondered why she felt such a tremor of dread pass through her. There wasn't time to think about it. A moment later, the car came to an abrupt stop in front of a yellow Victorian house with white trim.

"We're here," her mom said.

∞

The aunts were pleasant and welcoming, as Josie had assumed they'd be. Emily trailed behind as they toured the house, but Josie bounded forward and quickly pinpointed the kitchen as her favorite room in the house. It was an enormous room with white wood cabinets, yellow curtains, and a huge island sitting in the middle, which had been put in since the last time she'd visited. It held several mixing bowls, a mess of loose flour and sugar, and two large vases full of wildflowers, giving it the air of a modern-day witch's workspace.

"You'll have to excuse the mess," Aunt Joan said as she led them through. "Alice was intent on baking some goodies for you, and I'm afraid all she did was scatter flour everywhere."

"Not true, Joanie, I managed to get some chocolate chip cookies out of it," Alice said. She had appeared seemingly from nowhere and was using a dish towel to take a hot pan of cookies out of the oven. The entire house smelled divine.

Josie felt Emily move forward a bit as the scent of the cookies hit her. Chocolate was her little sister's weakness.

"Go ahead, dear, have one," Alice said, holding the pan out to Emily. "You can find them in the back of the mirror."

Emily stopped with her hand in mid-air as the entire group looked at Alice.

"What?" Emily asked. Immediately, she moved back to the comfort of Josie's shadow.

"Come on, then, I'll show you upstairs," Joan said, and swiftly ushered them all towards the stairwell on the other side of the kitchen, leaving Alice standing by the oven with a slightly confused look on her face.

"You'll have to pardon Alice," Joan said once they were out of earshot. "She had a minor stroke a few years back, don't you know. Sometimes she says the silliest things, but she never remembers it later. It's taken a toll on her memory, as well. Don't be scared, dears. She means well."

The sisters threw one another a look as their mother followed Joan up the stairs, and Josie did something she hadn't done in years: she took Emily's hand.

"These rooms don't get used much, but we opened the vents so they would be nice and warm, and there are clean linens on the beds," Joan said as the group reached the landing. There were three large bedrooms on the right, a bathroom on the left along with two rooms whose doors were closed, and what looked like a closet at the end of the hallway. "Alice and I moved to the ground floor last year because it gets harder and harder to climb these stairs with each passing season."

"It's lovely," Josie's mother said, surveying the first room. It boasted a huge fireplace with a carved mantel and a cherry canopy bed and matching nightstand; everything else had been removed. "I think I'll take this one, if that's alright."

Josie and Emily nodded their agreement, but it turned out that all three rooms were pretty much the same, minus the bed. A moving company would be bringing the girls their own furniture, which came as a relief.

Josie chose the room at the end of the hall, in part because it included French doors that opened onto a small terrace. She pulled them apart and stood on the balcony as her mother and Joan chatted about the antique canopy in her mother's room. The day was cold and cloudy and full of the scents of October; the smell of wet leaves was rich around the old house; someone was burning them nearby. Josie closed her eyes for a moment and conjured up Andy's face in her mind, letting herself remember the months just after his disappearance when all she could think about was how to get him back. Even though they were at their own home at the time, Josie had always felt like this house, or perhaps even the aunts themselves, held the key to where he'd gone. She often got the impression that her mother felt the same way. She'd never come out and said it aloud, but sometimes there was something in her eyes—a glimmer of hope, maybe—whenever she talked about the aunts or this house, as though deep, deep down she thought Andy had ended up back here somehow and was simply unable to get home.

Her memories from that summer were almost nonexistent, but something nagged at a corner of her mind like a dog worrying over a bone. Something about shadows...the Shadow Man?

"Josie?"

She turned to find Emily standing in the room behind her, a worried look on her face.

"What's up? Aren't these rooms cool?" Josie asked.

"I guess so."

"Em, what's the matter? Is it the new house? I know it seems big compared to the old one, but you'll get used to it. And I'm right next door."

"It's not the house," Emily said, not meeting Josie's eyes.

"Is it starting a new school? I'm not thrilled about it either, but maybe you can convince these kids that you were popular in Kentucky," Josie joked.

"Would you shut up?" Emily said with such vitriol that Josie actually took a step back. She had hardly raised her voice above a normal speaking level, but fear and frustration twisted it now into something barely recognizable.

"What's your problem?" Josie asked, frowning. "I'm just trying to help."

"I had a dream about Andy last night," Emily said, her lower lip trembling with the effort of keeping her composure. "I dreamed that the Shadow Man came for him, and I know you did too."

Chapter Three
The Shadow Man

Once, some centuries ago, there was a pale, slight boy who was never quite *there*.

He had been born a whole person who sometimes shimmered out of existence, but he always came right back. Of course, as he got older, things only got worse. When he got angry, for instance, he could make himself disappear at once just to make his mother worry. Having a horrible temper, he did this often, and at the age of four, he had gone away for an entire week. When he returned, his mother and father were so happy to see him alive that they weren't even upset with him. It was a lesson that stuck with him.

His parents were quite perplexed about his condition, and, being members in good standing inside their little village, they thought it best if no one knew about his affliction. There would be no schooling for him outside the home, and he wasn't allowed to be seen or to go outside at all. His parents told the other villagers that he had taken terribly ill and could have no visitors. The trouble was, the boy never felt ill at all. His affliction, as his parents called it, felt more like a talent as the years went by. As he began to move from boyhood into the body of a young man, he found he could control his abilities, although it was always difficult to dictate where he would end up.

Sometimes, when he disappeared, he would find himself in an unfamiliar town, in the middle of a crowded market full of good smells and the confusion of a lot of people talking at once. Other times he was by the sea, which he had never seen before and which he knew was far, far away from where he lived with his parents. Once he had opened his eyes to discover he was in a lavishly decorated, high-ceilinged room with ornate gold picture frames on the walls. The stone floors shone in stripes of late afternoon sunlight that slanted through the windows, although when he'd left home, it had been evening. Luckily, he was alone in the room because he knew his eyes were nearly goggling out of his head. His own home was a small, thatched-roof building with two rooms, as humble as all the others in his village.

Though he rarely found himself in the same place twice, he never spoke to anyone, and hardly anyone paid him any attention. He wasn't sure if it was luck or providence that kept him from "landing" in the middle of a crowded room where he would be easily noticed. The only thing he was sure of was that each place was vastly different from the last, not just in geography…but perhaps even in time.

One day, when the young man was in his nineteenth year, he found himself once more beside the ocean. He had left his own bed on a cold, windy night, and had opened his eyes on a warm summer day on the island of Mykonos. He smiled and listened to the sounds of the tide pounding onto the sand, lifted his head to breathe in deeply. Cautiously, he looked around for signs of other people and was somewhat surprised to see a woman kneeling on the sand some thirty yards away, holding an unconscious man in her arms. She didn't seem to notice him, so he walked closer, intrigued.

"I tried to help, but he was too far gone," the woman said without looking up. Her pale hand held the man's head to her breast, and she rocked back and forth as though soothing a baby.

She turned to look at him, her waist-length hair as dark and shiny as the underside of a crow's wing, and he saw tears in her eyes. "I couldn't help," she said. "Sometimes I can."

He knelt beside her and looked down at the man, who was clearly gone. "What happened?" he asked gently.

She turned to the dead man and placed a kiss on his forehead. "I came upon him flailing in the waves, but I couldn't reach him fast enough. By the time I pulled him out, he…" she trailed off and looked up, squinting against the bright sun to follow the path of a seagull as it darted over the waves, hunting for food.

"Are you alright, Miss?" he asked, touched by her willingness to risk her own life to help a man in trouble.

She gave him her full attention for the first time, her wide, pale eyes seeming to hold secrets he couldn't fathom. There was a sadness about her that he'd never seen in another human being.

He could only liken it to something that had happened to him on his first day of working on the farm, when he was asked to accompany the farmer into the woods to hunt for deer. It had been a cold day, and the evenings were getting longer, and the man wanted to lay by meat to dry into jerky that would take him through a rough winter.

They had walked into the stand of trees armed with bows and a quiver full of arrows each, although he wasn't a very good shot and had told the farmer so. The man said he didn't mind; he was more concerned about bringing back his catch—if he made one—and how heavy it would be.

After what seemed like a very long time, the farmer suddenly halted and held out a hand to stop him from walking. The two of them stood as still as a stone in the dusky glow of twilight, closing their mouths to keep clouds of their breath from escaping, and after a moment, he saw what the farmer had been sharp-eyed enough to see first: a large doe drinking from a puddle of rainwater. Quickly the man drew an arrow and, more silently than the boy could have done himself, nocked it in the bow. After a moment's hesitation, in which the man made a minute adjustment, he let loose the spear, and it buried itself into the soft fur of the doe's belly.

She ran. He would never forget the look of naked fear in her eyes before she turned, her white tail flipping a signal in the near-dark. They followed her, letting the glimmering trail of her blood lead the way, and after several minutes they came upon her lying in a clearing. She had lost too much blood and hadn't been able to run any more.

He looked away as the man pulled a long, thick branch from a nearby tree and produced two lengths of rope, but he knew he would have to help truss her up. He did so quickly and efficiently, not wanting to spend any more time on it than he had to. He had fished in the privacy of a nearby lake as a boy, but his father had never made him hunt, and now he was profoundly grateful for it.

They each took an end of the branch and swung it up onto their shoulders with the doe between them, hanging from her hooves. The arrow was still inside her; she was gone. The high, metallic smell of blood was all that remained of her in this place. They set off toward the farm, and after a few moments, something made the boy look back; he had spent the better part of the past year trying to forget what he saw there.

A young fawn, following them silently. Its eyes held the same look of loss and longing and confusion as the girl on the beach.

He looked at the girl now, at the curve of her eyes and the way she mourned so openly, and felt something stirring inside him that had never been there before. It was as though a cord connected the two of them, and he felt the oddest, most powerful sensation of sadness at the thought of breaking it.

"I'm alright," she said. "Sometimes, I forget that danger is what a seagull means to a clam."

She turned back to the ocean then, and he recognized the feeling in the pit of his stomach. It was the feeling one has upon finding a true matched soul, so rare in this life and so revered.

Chapter Four
A Confession

Josie lay awake in her new room, watching tree limbs shiver outside her window. October was a lot more chilly and damp in Maine than in Kentucky.

Looking around the room, she saw a lot of familiar things: her beloved book collection (the Harry Potter series took a place of pride on the mantel, secured by two carved wooden owl bookends), her easel and several glass jars full of brushes and paints, the twinkly Christmas lights she hung year-round at her window. Yet for all that was familiar, there was no comfort. All of her things had simply been transplanted into a new world, which served to make it all that much more unsettling.

She had known sleep wouldn't come easy, although the trip had exhausted everyone. That, coupled with the enormous meal of pot roast with potatoes and carrots that Joan and Alice had prepared, should have had her snoring and drooling into her pillow. Emily's confession had stunned her, then sent her mind spinning off in every direction.

Her little sister's sudden and uncharacteristic silence earlier in the day had been explained, but not much else had.

"I heard you talking in your sleep yesterday morning," Emily had said when the two of them were alone in Josie's room. "I had a horrible nightmare about *him*, and then I got up to go to the bathroom. When I walked past your room, I could hear you saying something about the Shadow Man. For a minute, I thought I was still dreaming." Her eyes darkened, and she turned to sit on the wide, cushioned window seat beside the balcony doors. "Who is he, Josie? How could we both be dreaming about him at the same time?"

Josie stood where she was, speechless. She only vaguely remembered her dream, but she knew she hadn't seen the man in question; Andy had said his name. She frowned at the memory and began to pace back and forth, something she always did when her mind felt too full.

"I don't know, Em," she said. "Until yesterday I'd never heard that name before in my life." Emily was gnawing on the edge of her thumb, something she hadn't done since she was very small when their parents had started slamming doors more and more often. It was a nervous gesture, but it also bespoke her regression to a habit from her early childhood, and Josie didn't like it. Not for the first time, she wondered if the move to Maine had been the right decision on their mother's part.

"Maybe we're not asking the right questions," said Emily, lifting her eyes to her sister's. They were ringed with the bluish circles of the perpetually exhausted, and Josie was startled to realize her little sister must have been having nightmares far longer than she'd let on. What else was she not telling her?

"What do you mean?" Josie asked.

"I mean, yes, we need to know who the Shadow Man is…but what does he have to do with Andy?"

Josie shook her head. "I wish I knew. I can't really remember my dream, but Andy was there. Something about a little door…and he said that name."

Emily gave a little sob and flung herself onto the window seat, burying her face in the soft cushions. "I don't like it here. I want to go home!"

Josie sat beside her sister and put an arm around her shoulders. "This is our home now, Em. We need to be strong for Mom, because as hard as this is on us, it's twice as hard for her. She didn't want to move us here."

"Then why did she?"

"She didn't feel like she had a choice. Dad didn't exactly do us any favors when he took off. Mom won't tell me anything about money, but I know there isn't much of it. It must be pretty bad if she felt like moving us here was the only way to get by."

Emily sat up and wiped her face. "Sometimes I hate him."

Josie nodded. "Yeah. Me too."

Emily turned to her, surprised. "You do?"

"Sometimes I think I'm over it, that it doesn't hurt anymore, and I can't be mad when the pain is gone. Then something will make me think of him, or I'll dream about the last time we saw him, and it will come rushing back. But mostly I hate him for what he did to Mom. He didn't just leave us, he left her. He left her alone to take care of everything, and I know he was upset over Andy, but she was too. He's a selfish jerk."

The day their father left, Josie was late getting home from school. She'd been helping her art teacher unload a crate of clay into her storeroom so the class could begin working on the potter's wheel, something Josie knew would exasperate and enthrall her in equal measure. Emily was at violin practice, and since her elementary school was just across from the high school, Josie stopped by when she was finished so they could walk home together.

Their mother was home, her car parked crookedly in the driveway. Josie immediately knew something was wrong and very nearly told Emily to stay outside on the porch while she went inside to investigate, but her little sister was already skipping ahead up the steps, blissfully unaware of Josie's sense of foreboding.

"His things are gone. Everything. He took his Honda and half the money in the checking account," their mother was saying into the phone in the kitchen. Emily threw down her backpack and began to rummage around in the pantry for a snack, but Josie stood in the doorway, watching her mother clutch her stomach with one arm as though she might be sick. She was pale, a fine sheen of sweat glistening on her forehead. When she made her excuses to get off the phone, she turned to Josie.

"I need to talk to you," she had said, and even though Josie knew what was coming, she felt dizzy with the reality.

That was almost exactly one year ago, and since then the three of them had clung to one another like unfortunate souls drowning in a massive undertow. At 14, Josie didn't have much awareness of what her mother's finances entailed or how a mortgage worked, but she knew things weren't looking good. Even with two jobs, Elizabeth Burns was struggling to pay the bills on time. Their electricity had been cut off more than once in that big old house, but it was always restored. Her mom kept her chin up, went to work without complaint, and never asked a soul for help.

Not that she had many people to ask. Her own parents were long dead, and she had no brothers or sisters. Her only living relatives were the aunts, and although she had finally given in to their invitation to come stay with them, it had taken some convincing. Elizabeth was much too proud to let anyone know she was struggling; in fact, Josie had wondered several times how they even knew about the dire situation in the Burns household, because her mom didn't speak to them regularly. They traded cards at holidays and birthdays, but that was about it.

Secrets, secrets. Their house practically whispered them through the halls, keeping them closed in and safe from outsiders. Sometimes Josie felt she would go to her grave never knowing her own mother, a woman she had lived with her entire life.

"Everything ok in here?"

Josie looked up to see her mom in the doorway, an expression of concern etched across her delicate features.

"Yeah, we're just talking. I was thinking maybe I could take Em downtown sometime, show her the library and stuff."

"That's awfully nice of you," Elizabeth said. "I'll be doing boring things like unpacking and cleaning for the next few weekends. You girls should go have some fun."

As Josie lay in bed trying to turn off her brain so sleep could take over, it occurred to her that maybe this house was the key to everything: Andy, the shared dream, and this Shadow Man. Deep down, she had always felt that there would be answers here; it was just a matter of finding them. Tomorrow morning before school, she decided, she would talk to the aunts and find out everything she could about Bedford and what exactly had happened the week that Andy disappeared. Her mother would be preoccupied with lunches and helping Emily get ready; it was the perfect time.

Satisfied with her plan, Josie turned over and went to sleep.

∞

There was no time to talk to the aunts.

Sometime in the night, a storm blew in and knocked the power out on half the block, throwing dozens of houses into darkness. Josie was yanked from sleep by a frantic Emily, who was yelling something about alarm clocks and being late. The sun was all the way up outside the window.

Josie sat up and groaned, realizing what must have happened when she spotted her blank alarm clock on the nightstand.

"What time is it?" she hollered to Emily, who was running back and forth between her bedroom and the bathroom with frantic energy.

"Seven-thirty!" Emily yelled back. "We missed the bus so Mom's gonna drive us but we have to hurry!"

And so it was that Josie began her first day of school in Bedford by sprinting across the school's front lawn, which was wet, and down the hallway which was not. Her trusty high-top Converse unfortunately provided no traction, so when she slipped on the slick tile, her feet kept going and her body followed. It wouldn't have been so bad if the door to her Language Arts class hadn't been open, affording her new peers a front-row view of her tumble. She skidded by the classroom like a baseball player sliding into home and heard the inevitable laughs follow.

"Miss Burns?" Her teacher, Mr. Alvarez, poked his head through the doorway just as she was pulling herself to her feet. He eyed her wet jeans and wind-blown hair with sympathy. "We've been waiting for you." Josie smiled to show that she was okay, hoping he would take the hint and not make a big deal out of her fall. Taking a deep breath, she straightened her hair and pulled her shoulders back. Fall or not, she wasn't about to show a class full of strangers her humiliation. Inside, several curious stares followed her to the only empty seat, along with a handful of snickers.

"What is she, homeless?" a blonde girl whispered to her friend, an obvious dig at Josie's mussed hair and ripped jeans. She kept walking, ignoring their giggles.

Mr. Alvarez sat on the edge of his desk and gestured to Josie.

"Class, this is Josie Burns. She comes to us all the way from Kentucky. Welcome to Bedford! I'm afraid I don't have a textbook for you just yet...ah, Miss Lee, would you mind sharing with Josie? And Josie, you just follow along as close as you can today and I'll get you a copy of the syllabus before the end of class."

The girl at the desk beside hers scooted closer, offering her open textbook so Josie could follow along as Mr. Alvarez began outlining the chapter. She wore three garnet studs in each ear, her shiny black hair straight as a pin. She smiled as Josie leaned in to read.

"I'm Alexa," she whispered. "I like this, did you draw it?"

She gestured to Josie's notebook, which displayed an inky fox in a snowy forest.

"Yeah," Josie whispered with a smile, thinking that maybe her first day wouldn't turn out to be a total bust.

Chapter Five
Andy

In New England, summer dies and autumn rushes in with glorious colors and smells. Trees sway their red and gold leaves in a macabre dance with the brisk wind, and the moon is fully risen by seven p.m. Darkness comes not on silent cat's feet, but seems to swoop down and draw heavy curtains across the sun.

But in the In Between, there were no seasons, not in the sense of summer and winter and spring and fall. Snow and heat lived side-by-side, showing up within days of each other. Time stretched on with nothing concrete to indicate its passing. It could be torturous to some, but Andy had grown used to it. In fact, he rather liked that no one around him aged, and the reflection he saw when he leaned over the poisoned waters of the Salacia River was unchanging.

At night, he often laid awake thinking about his old life, his stomach twisted into a slick knot with the worry that he might never see his family again.

The memory of his mom and dad and sisters was sometimes the only thing that got him through the days, but it was also the thing that brought him the most pain. Josie, especially, was on his mind. They had been so close, had shared so much when they discovered the In Between. But he knew she'd forgotten all about the world he now called home. He himself had started to forget almost as soon as they'd left Maine, but when he awoke to the sound of thundering hooves on the pavement—so loud he was certain the entire family would hear and run to his rescue—he remembered everything at once: the Shadow Man, the mirror, the universe he and Josie had found hiding inside the tiny cupboard in their aunts' basement. Some part of him had known that the Shadow Man would come for him eventually; what he hadn't been prepared for was how quickly it happened, and although he was happy Josie had been spared, a small piece of his soul—one he guarded viciously—wished that she had been brought here with him. At least they would be miserable together.

These rival thoughts chased one another in his head until he felt dizzy with them, until his insides felt as hard as stone. The only thing that made him feel halfway alive was sitting by the Salacia after the day slid into twilight, watching it flow endlessly west. The rainbow trout that snaked through the waves reminded him of the time his dad had taken him fishing; the two of them had sat on the banks of an anonymous river for most of an afternoon, not talking much and not needing to. Once again, it was a thought that both kept him going and kept him hurting.

He would be ten years old forever on the outside, but inside he felt like a man in the October of his years. He lay down on the river bank, exhausted, and was soon dreaming of the night he was taken from his own bed.

∞

Andy awoke from a nightmare in which he was drowning in a pool of murky water to the sound of shuddering hoofbeats that seemed to shake the pictures on the wall of his bedroom. He closed his eyes, willing it to be a continuation of his dream, and opened them to find the Shadow Man standing over him in the dark, his pale skin glowing in the dim moonlight filtering in through the window.

"Quickly, Andy, we must hurry," he whispered, and Andy shivered despite the sticky heat of his bedroom. The Shadow Man's voice seemed to go right through him, compelling him to move faster as he slid out of bed and pushed his numb feet into the nearest pair of shoes.

"Where are you taking me?" Andy asked, afraid of what the answer might be, but needing to hear the words.

"You know where we're going," the Shadow Man said. "You took something from me. And now you're going to show me where it is."

"But my mom and dad...I can't just leave," Andy said weakly.

"You can and you will," the Shadow Man said softly. His voice never betrayed his anger, but Andy could feel it shimmering in the room between them like heat over fresh blacktop. His limbs seemed to be moving of their own accord; it was akin to sleepwalking, except he was fully awake. His mind raced in a thousand directions, but none of them took him to an answer. He was in no position to fight someone as powerful as the Shadow Man.

Something moved in his closet.

The Shadow Man snapped his head around, but the door was closed, and there was nothing to see.

"Who else is in here?" he hissed at Andy.

"N-no one," Andy said, his words pulsing with the heartbeat in his throat.

Quickly, silently, the Shadow Man moved like smoke toward the closet and yanked it open. Stacks of baseball card books, board games, and magazines tottered in one corner; his clothes swayed with the movement of the door. That was all.

The Shadow Man closed the door swiftly and turned on Andy, who had been standing frozen beside his bed.

"Come," he ordered.

The carriage awaited them just outside, a gigantic black diligence at least thirteen feet tall. Six ebony steeds stood harnessed to the carriage, frothing at the mouth and pawing the ground impatiently. Their red eyes rolled around in their sockets, clearly from exhaustion. It had been a long trip from the In Between, and they had been ridden hard.

The Shadow Man had to lift Andy up into the carriage, and they took off into the night. There was no driver up front; the horses knew the path home and pounded their way through the quiet suburban streets without hesitation.

He would have never thought it possible, but exhaustion and fear tangled together and created a sort of sleep-elixir. His eyes felt as though someone had blown sand into them, so he closed them and felt himself being rocked into unconsciousness with the movement of the carriage.

When he woke up, the movement had stopped, and he was alone in the carriage. He sat up and looked out the window, wincing at the pain in his neck from the odd position he'd fallen asleep in. It was dusk in the In Between, and the horses had been unharnessed and were grazing in a small, scrubby field to the west of the Shadow Man's ebony castle. In the distance, pastel trees became brush strokes against the sunset.

The heavy iron doors were closed firmly against the cold, although The Guardians, Detrus and Grimble, were still standing silent sentry on either side. Carved from pure alabaster, The Guardians resembled the ancient gargoyles which decorate many old structures across Europe and had protected the castle for hundreds of cycles—a term In-Betweeners used instead of years. Andy eyed them warily, wondering if he should wake them and ask if he was expected to sleep outside. He decided against it, knowing he wouldn't be able to sleep for a long time anyway.

He wandered over to the field and leaned against the black horse-fence, wishing he could smell the grass the animals were grazing on. But everything was different in this world; the air was flat and carried almost no scents at all. The Salacia River flowed reddish-purple in the distance, shimmering in the glow coming from Mt. Orion. The peak of the mountain reached so high into the clouds that it was impossible to see from this distance. Andy knew no one had ever climbed it and lived to tell the tale.

"You, boy. What are you doing here?" called a gravelly voice.

Andy turned to find Detrus, the gargoyle who stood to the left of the castle doors, regarding him with a cautious look.

"The Shadow Man brought me," Andy replied, walking closer. He snuck a look at Grimble, who had the foulest temper of them both, but he was sleeping soundly.

"I know that. I just don't understand what you're doing standing here in one piece. I thought once Shadow found you, he would feed your thieving hide to the dogs."

"I'm not a thief," Andy said quietly. He had plenty of anger, but it wouldn't do to release it here.

"I daresay Shadow would argue to the contrary," Detrus said.

"Yes," Andy said. "He was pretty upset." The last word trembled on his lips and he swiped at his eyes, not wanting to appear weak in front of this ancient being.

"I'm willing to wager he has big plans for you, young man. Otherwise, you would be nothing more than a grease spot in your little human bed."

"What will he do with me? Why did he kidnap me in the middle of the night?"

Detrus, whose big stone face rarely changed, grumbled laughter. "Shadow didn't kidnap you, boy."

"Yes he did. He brought his carriage, the horses…"

"The Shadow Man can't travel outside of the In Between. He sent one of the thirteen ghosts to collect you."

Of course. He had forgotten. Andy swallowed, hard. It was like swallowing a lozenge.

"Thirteen ghosts," he whispered. The term clanged in his brain like a frenzy of church bells, but he couldn't place it.

"A group of spirits without faces," Detrus said. "All the more easy to disguise, and their services come at a high price. Shadow went to a lot of trouble to get you."

The sky was changing, swirling reds and blues that looked like the inside of a lava lamp. There was nothing here to remind Andy of home. He felt his throat constrict and pressed his hands to his eyes, wishing Josie was with him. She, at least, would have told him to stop being such a baby. But every-

thing that had happened was his fault. If they had never found that mirror…

The Shadow Man would never let him go home willingly. Andy thought back to their escape and wondered if Josie remembered anything at all about their time here. As soon as they'd returned home, he realized he was forgetting things. It was almost as though the In Between was a dream he'd had a long time ago; it was the sound of hoofbeats that brought it all back, and by then it was too late. Too late to warn Josie, too late to tell anyone about what they'd found hidden in the aunts' house during a game of hide-and-seek.

Part Two
Before

Chapter Six
The Discovery

"Come look what I found," Josie called.

Andy trotted downstairs, following the sound of his sister's voice, and found her standing in front of a towering pile of cardboard boxes. They weren't marked, but some of the ones on top were so full they had started to split at the sides. Andy could see old photographs and papers peeking out from these.

"Congratulations, you found a huge pile of junk! And you just gave away your hiding spot, dork," Andy said.

Josie swatted at him. "No, look. I tripped over a tennis racket and caught myself on these boxes, and I found this."

She stood aside and bent over, pointing to a small space between the boxes and a ratty old couch that had been left to the mice. Deep inside the crevice beneath the stairs, Andy could see something glowing dimly. He bent and peered inside, but it was too dark to make out what it was.

"Maybe it's a crack in the foundation, and the whole house is about to fall into a sinkhole," Andy offered helpfully.

Josie ignored him and began shoving the couch aside, leaving a puff of dust in her wake. "Help me," she said.

Andy sighed. His sister's curiosity never amounted to anything good, and he'd been tired of hide-and-seek anyway. What he really wanted to do was head back upstairs to his video games and a few of those chocolate chip cookies Aunt Alice had made the night before.

Josie looked up at him, her eyes bright with excitement, and he rolled his eyes. It was hard for him to say no when she had her mind set on something, if for no other reason than that she would never let it go. It would be easier just to help her.

He leaned his shoulder into the couch and shoved, sliding it away from the stairs. The two of them worked on moving the boxes, which was a feat in itself due to their precarious positions, and after several sweaty minutes of work, a small door came into view.

It was pushed back beneath the stairs, painted the same dingy yellow as the rest of the basement, and shaped like an arch. There was no handle.

"Huh," Andy said.

"I wonder why the aunts never come down here," Josie said softly, marveling at the door. "I mean, the rest of the house is so neat and clean…"

Andy looked around at the mountains of old books, boxes, and furniture and shook his head. He couldn't imagine Aunt Joan or Aunt Alice ever coming down here amidst the dust and mouse poop to do anything. It was a strange space, disconnected from the rest of the house, and he wondered when either of them had been down here last.

"Maybe they started storing stuff down here and forgot about it," Andy said. "Or maybe they just got overwhelmed. They're not young ladies, you know.""Maybe," Josie mused. She took a step closer to the door. "Or maybe there's something in here they want to keep hidden."

Andy laughed. "Yeah, like dead bodies. I bet they've been killing for years and no one ever knew because they're such sweet old ladies, with their chocolate chip cookies and their homemade laundry soap. No one would ever suspect."

"Exactly," Josie said. Andy gave her a skeptical look. "Really, Jo? I think you're bored. Maybe it's time to find something else to do."

"Why? Are you scared of what we'll find?"

"I'm not scared. I just don't see the point in staying down here with all this dusty junk when we could be upstairs doing something fun."

But he *was* a little scared. The basement was an odd place, and not just because of what was in it. The light was different down here. It filtered in through dusty ground-floor windows that were only half a foot long, and that was part of it, but there was something else. It was like walking under the shark tunnel at the aquarium, where the light came through water and made the world look wavery and less...there. Suddenly he wanted more than ever to go upstairs and forget what his sister had found.

Josie was looking at him knowingly. "Go on, then. I'm going to check it out."

Andy frowned. "Okay, fine. You can move these boxes back by yourself."

Smiling, she turned back to the door. She knelt on one knee in front of it, studying it for a moment. Then she brought one hand up and moved it along the seam of the door. Andy realized he was holding his breath and let it out, relieved. They wouldn't be going inside, after all, it seemed. With no door knob or handle—

But no. Josie pressed her fingers to just the right spot on the wood and the door popped open, as easily as if it had just been used.

Andy bent to look over her shoulder, his eyes widening as they took in what was on the other side. A little room was before them, barely big enough to hold two people, with a concrete floor and plain white walls. Inside sat a well-used blue blanket, a small wind-up alarm clock, and a gas lantern, which was lit. That was the source of the light they'd seen peeking through the crack in the door.

"What in the world?" Andy whispered.

Josie duck-walked into the little room and sat down inside, looking around in wonder. "Whose do you think it is?"Andy shook his head, genuinely at a loss for words. "I don't know who could have been in here with this lamp on when all those boxes were stacked in front of the door."

He shuffled forward and looked around, but there was nothing more to see except blank walls. Josie looked incredibly cheerful at their find, but everything about it bothered him. There was no easy explanation for it, and it made him uncomfortable. Like he'd just come across a secret he was never meant to know.

"Come on, let's go. I don't think we should be in here," he said.

"Wait, there's something here," Josie said. She pulled a dull pewter hand-mirror and a small blue book from beneath the blanket and held them up. The book was blank on the outside, but when she opened it up the pages were full of tiny, cramped black ink. A thin piece of black ribbon acted as a bookmark and held a small brass key, ornately carved at the top and fitted with a shimmering opal.

"Look at this," she said softly. "It's a list of instructions."

Andy's was uneasy about the room, but the prospect of finding some answers in what appeared to be a journal was too good to pass up. He leaned into the room and looked at the page, and he and Josie began reading it aloud together.

Stand arm to arm. While holding the mirror aloft, recite: I am the keeper of the book. I am the knower of things to be known. I was here once. I need to be shown. By the power of 2x2, hear my cry: VILLOU!

And that was it. From that moment on, their lives were forever altered. The words had transported them to the In Between, where they stayed for two entire days before they could figure out how to get back. When they returned—filthy, terrified, starving, and utterly exhilarated—Andy and Josie discovered they had only been gone about two hours. That was when they knew they had something special, something that was really real. The cupboard under the stairs didn't just take them to another world...it took them to another *when*, a world where the very definition of time as they knew it didn't exist. Andy's mind had been almost painfully alive with ideas when they returned, and he and Josie began staying up later and later into the night to talk about their plans. She wanted to go back immediately to figure things out, to see more of that world. It was so different and terrifying and enormous, full of purple lakes and trees with blooms that looked like pink candy-floss, but the knowledge that they had discovered something so huge trumped their fear. There was real, breathless magic around every corner.

Now, standing beside the river, Andy laughed at the memory, at how naive he had been. The visual delights of the In Between were just illusions, meant to draw in anyone foolish enough to go through that door.

When he and Josie made that first trip, they had been greeted by a girl with a pale, heart-shaped face and long black hair named Annika who quickly ushered them away from the portal and introduced them to other children from her world. She and Josie became close, and they spent so much time together that Andy was afraid Josie would suggest bringing her back home with them. But she never had the chance to, because the last time they had visited the In Between, they were faced with the Shadow Man and his anger, which was so fierce it left them breathless in its intensity.

Shadow was a fierce ruler, with many guards in his employ. They roamed the land, always on the lookout for anything out of the ordinary or anyone who might be engaging in some wrongdoing. The rules were blurry; Andy only knew that if a person was summoned to the castle, it would not end well for them. He had no idea why the Shadow Man even allowed others to live in the In Between, unless it was simply that he liked being a ruler. The land was dense, with rocky soil that was mostly untenable covering most of it. Gardens had been planted to sustain the citizens, but they weren't very reliable, and the vegetables that did grow were odd colors. Fortunately, Andy thought to himself, whatever it was about the In Between that dulled the air also affected appetite and the need for nutrition. Sometimes he would go for days without eating but never became hungry.

He was so homesick that even a reprimand from his sister would have been welcome. He had no idea how long he had been gone; would they be looking for him already?

Time, that elusive destructor, which someone somewhere once called "the old bald cheater". Andy had begun to realize just how apt that description was. After he lived here for a while, his outward appearance would remain the same, but emotionally and mentally, he would grow as any other boy would. He had seen the effects of time in the In Between and knew he had a long, tiresome road ahead of him, and he would walk it alone.

Chapter Seven
Down Below

The air smelled like secrets and soot.

Down below, where the only light was dull and gray, Shadow moved surefooted and confident. It had been months since he'd visited the dungeons, which were now empty, but he still knew every passage like the back of his hand. It was cold, far too cold for a person to be comfortable for very long, and he drew his robes around him tightly. Ordinarily, he wouldn't be down here at all, but one of the guards had relayed some very interesting information that afternoon, and Shadow wanted to see it for himself.

He rounded a corner and came to stand before three tunnels, each pitch black and emitting their own very particular scents: the first, cinnamon and clove; the second, sulfur and pine; the third, hay warmed by sunshine. He breathed in deep with his eyes closed, basking in the powerful memories they brought up and trying to picture what lay on the other side of each tunnel.

He inhaled again, eager to experience the pleasures of his sense of smell. The air around his territory was stale and held only a fraction of the olfactory delights of the World; Detrus and Grimble, who had been here longer than any living thing, had told him that. Those smells meant these portals, which had been a closed and silent secret in all the time Shadow had lived here, were open.

Shadow leaned as close as he dared, trying to ascertain whether he could feel the slightest touch of a breeze or hear any sound coming through. All was still.

"M'Lord?"

Shadow turned to find his High Guard, Rolo, standing in the arched doorway. His enormous frame nearly filled it. He was dressed inconspicuously today in black robes with a heavy hood that covered his horns. Golden eyes peeked out from its depths. Part human, part demon, part something Shadow couldn't define, Rolo was one of his most feared guards. Never afraid to hold someone by their heels over the poisonous river to get an answer out of them, never too busy to snap to attention when Shadow needed his assistance.

"Yes?"

"I conducted a sweep of the other tunnels, as you ordered. All is clear."

"Rolo," Shadow said slowly. "Did you know there were portals down here before today?"

Rolo shook his head slowly. He was a fierce creature and was extremely loyal, but he was not the brightest star in the sky. He was incapable of lying. "No, m'Lord."

"And you've never heard anyone speak of these tunnels in particular?"

"No, sir."

Shadow ran a hand through his unruly black hair, a thoughtful gesture that he had carried over from the World. "Tunnels disguised in plain sight, perhaps. This is old magic. Who was the first child to come here, in the early days?"

Rolo looked down at the rough stone floor, thinking. "I believe it was Annika, m'Lord."

Shadow scrolled through his memory files and came across a dark-haired girl with a pale, fragile face. If he recalled correctly, she had run away from Moscow in the early 1900s, unwilling to be a slave in her uncle's home after her parents died of illness, and had found herself here. And, like almost all lost souls who ended up in the In Between, leaving became harder and harder to do. As the years passed by in her world, Annika physically remained a 13-year-old girl. She was much like a prisoner who had been given a life sentence; after so many years in captivity, the thought of returning to the outside world was terrifying and impossible.

"Annika," Shadow whispered. "Fetch her for me."

∞

At the same moment, Shadow was inspecting the newly opened tunnels, Annika was a half-mile away from the castle, sitting on the banks of the beautiful, poisonous Salacia River with her new friend Josie.

Though she had only known the girl for a short time, Annika already felt as close to her as a sister. Perhaps, she reflected as she braided strands of pink tree floss into Josie's hair, it was because Annika had been in the dungeons when Josie and Andy came through the portals the first time. She felt responsible for them, in a way, and she longed for someone to love. The In Between was often a lonely place, even though its population had grown in recent years. Annika estimated there were more than 100 families who lived here, their homes scattered around the vast landscape with the Shadow Man's castle at the center. Yet she remained alone, living in a small one-room house she had constructed with the help of some of the others. The entire community kept and worked several large fields which supplied wheat, vegetables, nuts, and fruit, and everyone shared the bounty. Yet for all their collaboration, each group kept to themselves for the most part. Annika didn't even know where most of them had come from or why they had ended up in the In Between. Despite some friendships with a few of the younger residents, hers was a solitary life, and always had been.

She often sneaked into the lower levels of the castle on quiet days, in part because the rough stone floors and cool, slightly damp walls reminded her of her old home. It was dark and quiet down there, and on hot days she sought refuge in the shadowy passages which smelled of soot and quartz.

On the day she met Josie and Andy, she had been meandering slowly through the tunnels with no particular destination in mind, trailing her hands along the stone walls, mindful of the section with the large loose brick so as not to pinch her fingers. It had been an ordinary day, a rather boring one, until at length she reached a familiar section of passages that were usually too dark to enter. This time, one of the three tunnels was lit with a faint blue light, and when she breathed deep, she could smell the powerful scent of cookies.

Curious, she stepped a little closer and felt the unmistakable shimmer of magic in the air, tingling her fingertips and standing the fine hairs at the back of her neck on end. She took a step back, and a moment later, two children tumbled through the tunnel's entrance. Annika stared with eyes that felt as large as dinner plates, watching as the children—a boy and a girl—stood up and looked around warily.

"Hello," she said breathlessly as she stepped forward from the shadows, and they smiled in return.

"Hi," the girl said. "What's your name?"

The boy was goggling at his new surroundings with his mouth hanging open, and Annika could see that he was going into shock.

"I'm Annika," she said. "Where did you come from?"

"Maine," said the girl. She was looking around as well, but didn't seem as fazed by it all as the boy did.

Thoughts spun through her head so quickly she could barely catch one; she only knew that she didn't want the Shadow Man to know these children had come through the tunnel. Some nearly forgotten instinct told her that it would be very, very dangerous for them if he did.

"Come," Annika said, reaching out a hand for the girl to take. "Let's get you someplace safe."

And the children—brother and sister, Annika learned within the next few minutes—had followed her out of the dungeons as she led them expertly through the tunnels and out the small hole in the North wall that served as her door. As far as she knew, no one else knew about it; this end of the castle was never used anymore, as the Shadow Man's living quarters were on the other side, and the guards only made occasional sweeps of the exterior.

So far, she had kept them safe and untouched by Shadow and his men, but only, she was sure, by pure luck. If they ever came through the passage while someone else was down there the secret would be out, and because time worked so differently in the World, they couldn't coordinate their visits with her.

Annika didn't want to expose them to any danger, but there was a little part of her that was loath to tell them to stay away. She hadn't felt such a connection to anyone here in more than fifty cycles; knowingly sending Josie away never to return was a thought she couldn't bear.

She looked down at Josie, whose head was in her lap, and stroked her hair gently. Annika knew she was being unreasonably selfish, but her heart and her brain wanted two different things.

"Annika?" Josie asked drowsily, her eyes closed.

"Hmm?"

"How did you get here? Did you come through the tunnel like we did?"

Annika shook her head. "I didn't come through a tunnel. I ran away from my home because…well, it's a bit complicated, but I wasn't happy there. My parents died from fever, so I left. I knew people would be looking for me, so I went someplace that was sure to have lots of hiding places…the woods. The trouble was, I hid so well I got myself good and lost. I wandered for two days, and by that time, I was so hungry and tired, I probably wouldn't have minded if my uncle came and found me and dragged me back to his home. On the second night, I was looking for a place to camp when I fell into a large hole in the ground deep within a stand of trees. I thought I had broken my ankle, but when I stood up, I found it supported my weight. And I also saw, much to my surprise, that I wasn't in the same forest anymore. I was here, on the other side of a portal."

Josie was looking up at her with wide, interested eyes. "Has anyone else ever come through that way?" Annika shook her head once more. "The Shadow Man sent his men to the World to find all the portals and close them long ago. He said he didn't want any more outsiders here."

Josie swallowed. "I guess that means us, too."

Annika opened her mouth to answer, but was distracted by the sight of her friend Alek running toward them at full speed.

"Alek?" she said. "What's wrong?"

The teen stopped on the bank, his chest heaving from exertion. "Shadow…is looking for you. Tomas overheard Rolo askin' around about you…I think he knows you was down in the dungeons."

Annika extricated herself gently but firmly from Josie and stood up, looking at the castle as if she expected Shadow's men to appear there in a mob. Alek and Tomas were brothers and were the only people who knew she sometimes roamed the tunnels…largely because they had been known to explore the dungeons themselves. They were towheaded and mischievous, but they had been in the In Between nearly as long as she had and she trusted them implicitly.

"How does he know?"

Alek shook his head.

Annika bit her lip. "Will you take Josie to her brother, please, and get them safely to the tunnel? It's imperative that they leave at once."

"Of course," Alek said, taking Josie by the hand. "Where will you go?"

"I'm going to fetch a cloak and see if I can get close to the castle without anyone spotting me. I want a look at Shadow before he knows I'm there."

"Annika, don't go!" Josie said tearfully. She pulled away from Alek and threw her arms around Annika's waist. She had never seen the Shadow Man thanks to Annika's interference, but she knew that everyone feared him, and the fact that he was looking for her friend drew a bubble of anxiety into her throat.

Annika pried Josie's arms away gently and crouched down a bit to look into her eyes. "I have to go, *vozlyublennaya*. Promise me you'll go back through the portal with Andy as soon as you can. I need to know you'll be safe."

Josie nodded and allowed Alek to lead her away, looking back over her shoulder as they went.

Annika, who had never drawn Shadow's wrath before, realized that was about to change.

Chapter Eight
The Man Before the Shadow

The Shadow Man, who once answered to the name Revel in far simpler times, was a study in paradoxes.

His hands were long-fingered and graceful, yet he could never quite keep a grasp on anything fragile. His dark eyes seemed to hold all the secrets of the universe when the light hit them, and then one could see rings of blue and gold, like striations on the surface of a distant planet.

Perhaps the most intriguing thing about Shadow was his ability to be both patient and impatient, a man who could sit in the same position for hours and meditate, yet nearly come unhinged when he was waiting for something (or someone). He was not a person to be kept waiting, and he was most definitely not the sort one would ever steal from. He was more than an average man and was not to be underestimated; he had glimpsed things most humans had only ever read about; he had seen into other worlds and other times, and he had come back assembled as a whole, perhaps made even better by his experiences.

But those same experiences had also altered him. He was now unrecognizable from the young man who had once helped a farmer carry a doe through the woods. He had lived for so many years without a country of his own, skipping from existence to existence in the months after the death of his parents and before he met Penelope, and it had left a shadow on him. When he lost her, well...as the romantics say, everything lost meaning. The world went dark and so, too, did his heart. He had time to mourn the loss because it seemed to him that until he met Penelope; he was only going through the motions of being human. After she came into his life, he felt less like an imposter and more like he had found something that made him feel truly alive. Without her—and banished from the World to live in the In Between because he had fallen in love—he was ashes in the shape of a man.

He sat in his library, surrounded by ancient texts and fantastical, leather-bound books which had been printed in other worlds, and reflected. His anger at being bested by a child was still bubbling just beneath the surface of his skin, and he wasn't quite ready to face the boy; he was aware that his temper might overcome him, that he might do something stupid and irreversible to Andrew, and then all this would have been for nothing. Shadow didn't feel the need to hurry. Instead, he leaned back in the expansive leather chair beside the floor-to-ceiling window, set the metronome, and closed his eyes. He wasn't in the mood to meditate; when he found himself with a particularly difficult problem, meditation only made him anxious.

But oftentimes allowing himself to slip into a near-sleep, hovering over the border, with one foot in this world and one foot in the land of dream, calmed him and allowed his overfull mind to focus. It was as close to traveling as he could get these days, and as he felt himself grow heavy with relaxation, the smell of old books and cracked leather faded. In a moment, he found himself thinking of Penelope.

The metronome ticked and tocked, a steady rhythm that kept pace with his heart.

∞

Penelope was beautiful, with eyes the color of the sea right before a storm and hair so black and glossy it seemed spun from pure silk. Revel had never dared to imagine that goddesses existed before he came upon Penelope on the beach that day, but he did believe in angels. If they walked the Earth, he thought, then she must be one.

Having lived such a sheltered life, Revel hadn't given much thought to falling in love. The concept was not lost on him; after all, his mother and father had loved one another very much, and Revel assumed that most people eventually found their compliment and married them. But he was different. Traveling as he did, without knowledge of where he was or how he'd gotten there, did nothing to broaden his horizons or help him soak up culture, and he certainly never met anyone on those trips. Until Penelope.

She was elusive in so many ways, answering his questions about her past with only a little smile before changing the subject. She seemed hesitant to open up and love him back, even after months of him courting her, although it wasn't that she was cold; quite the opposite. He had never imagined such warmth and kindness even with his own mother as the model to which he held Penelope up.

Despite his lack of worldly experience, Revel was not dimwitted; he understood that the death of his parents—two months apart—had left him with a large hole in his heart that he might be unconsciously looking to fill. He had no doubts about the validity of his love for Penelope, however. From the day they met, Revel was taken. He hadn't been back home, hadn't traveled anywhere since she'd come into his life. That first week, he slept on the beach and waited for her to meet him during the day. After many months, they were married by the local justice, and he moved into her home, a lovely and humble shack near the water that she had decorated in seashells. Their days were full of sun and laughter; at night, they had fish and buttery crab and mussels for dinner and went to sleep with heavy bellies and happy hearts. Revel would wake in the morning and wrap his arms around Penelope, breathing in the comforting scent of the beach in her hair and wondering in the back of his mind when it would all be taken from him. Surely something this pure and good couldn't last.

When she became pregnant the next year, Revel couldn't keep himself from imagining that everything would turn out alright for them; there was simply no other option. Penelope was a second heart living outside his body, and their baby would be a third. It was only when the locals began avoiding them that Revel caught a whiff of something, a darkness that he could never quite grasp.

"Why do you think they've stopped talking to us?" he asked Penelope one evening over dinner. That afternoon had been a difficult one, with tension swirling around at the open-air market they shopped at. What had once been curious stares were now openly hostile, with one woman even going out of her way to fork the sign of the evil eye at them.

She gave him a sad smile and shook her head minutely, patting her rounded stomach. "It doesn't matter, love. We have everything we need right here."

"But it matters to me," Revel said. "I want you and our child to have the best life possible. It isn't fair to make you stay in a place where people treat you badly."

"I won't leave," she said firmly. It was the first time she had ever spoken so strongly, and he recoiled a bit.

"Penelope. Please tell me what's going on."

She sighed and pushed her plate away. "I don't like talking about it."

"Did something happen? You know I can't protect you if you keep secrets from me."

"I didn't want to hurt you," she whispered, and as she began to cry, Revel felt his pulse speed up. "The first day we met, that man I was trying to help…he was someone I loved."

Blood rushed into Revel's ears. "What?"

"Tristan. I knew him for a long time before that day. We were going to run away together, and I foolishly told my sister, Despoine, about our plans. She was jealous, furious that I had found someone I loved while she had no one. She ran straight to my father and told him what I was going to do, and he knew there was nothing he could say that would change my mind. He has had plans since before I was born to marry me off to a specific family so that I could bear him a grandchild with a powerful name, but that wasn't what I wanted. I fell in love with someone else, so he took care of the problem in his own way: he lured Tristan into the water and drowned him in the waves."

Revel took Penelope's hand. "My god."

"I'm sorry I wasn't honest with you about who Tristan was. I was heartbroken, and I couldn't imagine ever finding love again. After your kindness helped me heal, I started to fall for you in spite of it all. But I couldn't bring myself to tell you about what had happened. It was selfish of me. I didn't want to lose you."

"Penelope, I need you to tell me: are we in danger?"

She laid her head in her hand. A thick sheaf of hair fell over her shoulder as she did so, and Revel caught the scent of sand and sun and brine. "I don't know. I began to hear whispering among the locals several days ago. It seems they know who I am. None of them want to be associated with me because they're all terrified of my father and what he might do."

Revel frowned. "I don't understand. Why should they know who your father is?"

Penelope looked up with a smile as sad as he had ever seen. "Because he is Poseidon, God of the Sea."

Poseidon, God of the Sea, brother of Zeus, Keeper of the Waves. He was a being with many titles and of much-inflated ego and temper, who would fling his fury to the farthest corners of the universe on a whim. At the sound of his name, Revel felt a small vine of fear begin to wrap itself around his heart. He recalled that day on the beach, the day he had met Penelope and altered the course of his life forever.

"You said you were trying to help him," said Revel. "I didn't understand then what you meant, but you were trying to bring Tristan back, weren't you?"

Penelope closed her eyes. "Yes."

"You'd done it before? To someone else?"

"Once, for a little boy who was very ill. He had eaten a handful of wild berries and poisoned himself. His mother was hysterical, the doctors didn't know what to do for him and he was on the edge of death."

Revel sat silent for a moment, drinking it all in. "You're a goddess?"

"A demigoddess. My mother was a mortal."

"Is your father looking for you?"

She squeezed Revel's hand once, then twice, a comforting gesture as old as their relationship, and he responded despite the anxiety gnawing his stomach.

"I don't know," she answered simply.

Chapter Nine
Annika

The light was beginning to seep out of the day when Annika made it to the castle, heavily cloaked and hooded to discourage any passerby from talking to her. It stood just ahead, towering over her atop a hill, looking down on the land Shadow reigned over. She crouched behind a tree, wishing for the day to hurry up and lengthen to give her more cover.

Movement caught her eye, and she turned to see Andy at the bottom of the hill, standing at the fence to stroke the muzzle of a white horse. Her heart caught in her throat, and she ran to him quickly, still bent over to make herself as small as possible.

"Andy!" she hissed. "What are you doing here?"

He turned to her and smiled when he recognized her beneath the cloak. "I come here sometimes to feed the horses. We used to live near a farm back home, and my dad would take me riding—"

"Andy, you have to leave. Now."

He heard the urgency in her voice and moved away from the horse, his smile fading. "Why?"

"The Shadow Man has sent his men to find me and question me about something. I think they've found the tunnels. You and Josie are not safe right now. I sent her with Alek to find you so you can take her home."

Andy's eyes widened. "How will we get through if he knows the portal is there?"

"Follow me."

∞

Annika led Andy up the hill, keeping close to the trees to earn as much cover as possible. The day was growing chilly, and she drew the cloak around her, hoping silently that Alek had done his job and that Josie was waiting for them.

Through the small hole in the North wall and into darkness the two of them crept, ears attuned for anything at all. Annika took Andy's hand, and he looked down at them, clasped so easily, and gave a little squeeze. The calm in his touch betrayed the stutter of his heart against the cage of his ribs.

"Stay here," Annika whispered when they came to a crossroads within the tunnels. They had encountered no one, but she knew that the guards, as large and imposing as they were, could be completely silent when they needed to be. It would serve them well to be overly cautious. She crouched down and crab-walked an inch further into the gloom. To her left was a drafty, empty corridor; to her right was the direction of the portals, and she could see Alek's pale head bowed as he waited. Josie was a dim shape at his side. She reached back for Andy's hand and pulled him along, walking quickly but silently toward her friends.

"Alek," she breathed. "Thank you for getting Josie here safely. I owe you a massive debt."

He smiled, and Andy could see the color in his cheeks even in the cloudy light. "No debt, Miss Annika. I was happy to do it. Be safe."

His slim form slipped down the tunnel without a sound, leaving the three of them to say their goodbyes. Annika reached for Josie and pulled her close as Andy looked uneasily over his shoulder. Suddenly, despite his growing love for the In Between, all he wanted was to go back toward the smell of fresh-baked cookies and forget this adventure.

"It isn't safe for you here anymore, but this isn't goodbye," Annika said, her eyes shining in the gloom. "I'm certain we'll meet again. Get home safe, little lamb."

"I want to stay here with you, Annika. I don't understand! Why isn't it safe?" Josie asked pleadingly.

"Because you didn't ask permission to come into my house," a cool voice answered from behind them.

Annika whipped around to find the Shadow Man standing at the mouth of the tunnel with a large, cloaked guard. Golden eyes shimmered beneath his hood.

"Please, m'lord," Annika said evenly. "Your quarrel is with me. They stumbled through a portal, and I brought them into the In Between. If not for me, they would have gone back without ever having set foot outside the castle walls."

"That's an interesting tale, Annika, but as I had every portal sealed up ages ago, it doesn't interest me. Rolo, seize them."

Annika leapt in front of Andy and Josie but found herself swatted easily away by Rolo, who was several feet taller than she. One of his hands was bigger than her torso. He grabbed the children and pulled them away from the portals roughly. Something metal clattered to the stone floor, garnering Shadow's interest.

"What's this?"

He bent and picked up a small, cloudy hand mirror that had fallen out of Andy's pocket. The surface was cracked and not much use at all, Annika could see. The edges were dull gold flashing in the gray.

"Just a bit of glass I found," Andy said, but he was fooling no one. Annika could hear the blind panic in his voice even as he tried to tamp it down.

"Just a bit of glass," Shadow repeated, measuring him carefully with his gaze. "What does it do?"

Andy squirmed in Rolo's grip and shot a look at Annika, who stood by helplessly. "It does nothing. I found it in my grandmother's house."

Shadow walked forward, his pale skin a beacon as he used his gaze to enchant. Annika found herself suddenly unable to move, frozen in place by his gaze.

"You found a useless piece of looking glass and decided to keep it. Ah, the wonders of boyhood," Shadow said with a little laugh. Rolo rumbled briefly out of duty.

Josie was torn between watching Shadow and glancing meaningfully at Annika, hoping to catch her eye. Why wasn't she doing anything? She shifted slightly, moving her weight to the right, hoping the movement would catch Annika's attention. Rolo tightened his grip.

"Perhaps I should turn out your sister's pockets to see what other treasures you've brought into my home," Shadow said.

"She doesn't have anything," Andy insisted.

"So you say, but still, I think Rolo should hang her up by her small, perfect feet. Then we shall see what she carries."

"No!" Andy cried, twisting away from the giant guard. His efforts earned him a turned wrist, and he howled in pain.

Shadow walked forward slowly. "Tell me what the mirror does."

"It lets me travel!" Andy shouted. "When I'm home, it lets me travel anywhere I want. All I have to do is say the right word."

Shadow stopped. His face changed, almost imperceptibly, and Annika frowned. This wasn't right, she knew, but she couldn't quite place the why.

Shadow held the mirror up to his face and seemed to regard it with new eyes. "Tell me," he said. "Tell me what to say."

"M'lord...are you sure you should?" Rolo asked softly.

"Shut up! Tell me what to say, boy, or I'll have my guard snap your sister's neck!"

"Villou!" Andy cried. "Say, Villou!"

Shadow glanced at him, hard, and returned his attention to the mirror. After a moment's hesitation, he repeated the word...and disappeared.

"M'lord?" Rolo said.

He was gone. Annika shook her head slightly, as if to clear it, and saw a ghostly hand snake out of the gloom near her foot. It left a small vial of something red and then retreated before she could give away its presence, and suddenly she understood.

The guard was so shocked to find only empty air where Shadow had been that he stood slack-jawed, his grip loosened just enough on the children for them to wriggle free, she saw. She only had one chance to get it right.

"Rolo? I have something here you should see," Annika said, and moved forward quickly, shouting at the children as she did so to get out of the way. The moment she threw the vial of Salacia water in his face, he roared, dropped the arms of his prisoners, and stumbled back into the wall. The tunnels shook with his weight, shaking powdery granite dust down upon their heads.

"Andy, GO!" Annika screamed, and watched with relief as he grabbed Josie's hand and threw himself into the portal, pulling his sister behind him.

A blinding flash of blue light temporarily lit up the tunnel, and Annika turned her head, shielding her eyes within the din of Rolo's roaring. It was the Shadow Man, back from his travels already. He appeared directly in front of her and landed on both feet with a thud, eyes and hair wild as though he had been through a windstorm. Pebbles rained down upon them, and Annika began coughing uncontrollably as dust filled her mouth.

The mirror slipped from Shadow's hand and fell to the stones, where it cracked. Annika covered it with her foot and kicked it gently behind her, out of his reach. In the melee he never noticed.

"What is happening?" Shadow shouted. He seemed almost drunk, swaying on his feet, trying to make sense of the world he'd only just left that was now falling to pieces.

Rolo stumbled out of the shadows and laid a heavy hand on Shadow's shoulder; Annika could see angry red bubbles forming on his face, blistering beneath the now-ragged cloak. A crash like thunder rolled the floor, and she struggled to stay upright; Rolo's stumbling had caused a shift in the tunnels and they were collapsing around them. More dust flecked down into her hair, the quartz flakes glittering on her shoulders like dead stars.

"She poisoned me! Threw it in my eyes, m'lord!"

Shadow's own eyes narrowed. "Then you'll understand when I leave you here to die a coward's death."

He spun around, grabbing Annika by the shoulders and throwing her at Rolo. Larger rocks were falling like a hard sleet now, ticking off her bare arms and leaving streaks of blood where they made contact. She could barely see, but she knew Shadow was getting away, running down the last open tunnel to the exit. And as the rocks became boulders, and the world fell on Annika, she had a moment to hope that Alek had made it out alive, and that he knew how grateful she was for saving her life...no matter how brief a reprieve it was.

Chapter Ten
Poseidon

Four weeks before Penelope was due to give birth, Revel woke in the night to see flames licking at the bedroom window. Penelope's side of the bed was empty and cold, and he swung his legs from beneath the blanket to hit the ground running, blindly pushing back the panic that had begun to rise in his throat.

Outside, the darkness of two a.m. was illuminated in oranges and reds as a wooden pyre burned openly on the sand just outside the hut. Some of the logs had tipped over, spraying sparks onto the thatched roof; this was the cause of the flames Revel had seen outside the bedroom window. Down the beach, Penelope was running into the water to fill a bucket.

"Penelope!" Revel called. His panic had been tamped down somewhat at the sight of her face; she was safe. He ran to her as she struggled through the wet sand with the bucket, clutching her belly as she went. "What happened?"

"I couldn't sleep, and I was sitting in the rocking chair reading when I saw someone run by the window," Penelope panted, sobbing. "It was one of the villagers, he set the fire. What will we do?"

Revel took her in his arms and turned to watch the flames as they engulfed the shack, black smoke billowing toward the heavens. "We're alive. That's all that matters."

Penelope pulled away. "What do you mean? We're going to have a baby! The villagers know who I am and they want us gone. We have no home, no clothing, nothing of our own!"

The idea of traveling occurred to him like a match lit in the wind. He had never attempted to travel with another person, wasn't even sure it was possible, and he would never endanger Penelope and their child that way. He pulled her gently down the beach, further away from the fire. "I promised you I would take care of you and our child, and I will. Tonight, we'll walk to the nearest farm and find a safe place to sleep, and when the sun comes up, I'll hire a carriage, and we will leave this place." Penelope shook her head in despair. "Where will we go? You don't understand, Revel. No place is safe, not forever. Sooner or later, people will figure out who I am, or my father will catch up to me, and we'll have to run again. I'm tired of running, my love. I'm so tired."

Revel could feel anger bubbling up inside his chest. What did she want him to do, rebuild their home in the ashes and pretend the villagers didn't want them dead?

"I will not keep you and our child in danger," he said firmly. "Perhaps we should seek out your father and have a talk with him."

"No!" Penelope cried over the pounding surf, grabbing his hands in a pleading gesture. "You can't do that! He'll kill you!"

"I won't be intimidated. This has gone far en—"

Revel stopped in mid-sentence, watching the sea over Penelope's shoulder. The waves had been coming hard and fast, pushed roughly ahead of a coming storm that he could smell on the air, and now they began to rise to towering heights. The swells were at least forty feet high, building strength and gathering speed, and now he could see something bright in the center of the tallest one. A blue light, becoming more and more intense as the wave moved closer to shore.

"Penelope," he said hoarsely. "We have to leave."

She turned, eyes wide, her entire body thrumming with fear. "No," she whispered.

Lightning streaked toward the water, splitting the sky and illuminating the churning sea. Riding the wave with a golden triton in one massive hand, Poseidon skated toward them on the surface of the water, pushing the surf to either side of him as he came. Revel moved in front of Penelope and stretched his arms out to shield her, walking slowly backward as he did.

The god of the sea was fiercely intimidating at well over eight feet tall, with bright blue eyes that burned cold as revenge or hot as murder depending on the moment. A long white beard gleamed in the firelight, not quite obscuring a strong chin and an expression of rage. He stood on the sand in dark robes that gave him the air of a judge. And perhaps, Revel thought, that's what he was.

"Penelope," he boomed. "It's been too long, daughter."

Revel could feel Penelope edge around him slightly. "How did you find me?"

"Your sister is still a talented tracker."

"Despoine," Penelope said through her teeth.

"She's been watching you for weeks, whispering to the villagers about you," Poseidon said. "As I'm sure you remember, Despoine is quite influential when she wants to be."

He looked pointedly down the beach at the hut which was completely engulfed in flames and would likely attract attention at any moment. With a flick of the triton, a great glut of water fell from the sky directly onto the fire, extinguishing it with a sizzling sound.

"Why do you insist on running from your destiny?" Poseidon asked, turning back to Penelope.

"Your destiny, you mean," Penelope spat. "Everything you've ever wanted for me was to benefit you and your plans. You have never cared about me."

"How dare you," Poseidon said, and his tone was dangerous. Revel could feel the tiny hairs on the back of his neck stand up. "You have forced my hand time and time again. Do you think I enjoy chasing you across the world? Do you think I would engage in this ridiculous game if I didn't care about you?"

"My life is not a game!" Penelope cried boldly, stepping out beside Revel to fully face her father with a protective hand beneath her belly. "Revel and I are married and we are going to start a family. It's too late for what you want. And you will never see your grandchild, not if I have anything to say about it."

"What about what I have to say?" asked a smooth voice from behind Penelope.

Revel whirled around to find a dark-haired woman standing with her arm curled around Penelope's neck. His wife, his love, was trapped. Her crystalline eyes widened with pure terror; he watched as her mouth formed his name, wanting to rush forward and pull her free, but every move was stretched out, as though he were walking through quicksand. Despoine smiled, winked, and with a silvery flash, disappeared into the night and took Penelope with her.

"No!" Revel screamed, and time seemed to speed up once more as he wrapped his arms around empty air.

"She's gone," Poseidon said. "The question now is, what to do with you?"

Revel turned to the god, feeling pure hatred burn through every blood vessel of his body. When it reached his mouth, he tasted ash and darkness.

"Bring her back," he said. A funny thing had happened to his voice; rage and pain had turned it into something unrecognizable, even to himself.

"I'm afraid that's not possible."

"Bring her back to me now," Revel said, moving closer.

A sudden blinding pain shot through his head and he fell to the ground, writhing in agony. It was what he imagined a sword through the brain felt like, a silvery blade that blotted out the rest of the world. He screamed, but the sound was swallowed by the waves as they cranked up again. Thunder began to rumble in the distance. Or was that inside his head?

"I can make the pain stop," Poseidon said from above him. "I can make it all go away, memories and all. Just say the word, and I'll send you into your next life."

Revel grasped his head; the pain was so great he could see colors swirling behind his eyes. Flashes of Penelope's face appeared with each strike of lightning over the ocean: the way she'd looked the first day they met, so fragile and beautiful, the look in her eyes when she had told Revel she was going to have a baby. He couldn't give up his memories of her, no matter how much it cost him.

"Never," he gasped.

The storm began to pick up. He could smell brine and smoke on the wind and wished to be back in his bed, dreaming all of it. After a moment, he saw Poseidon's robes come into view.

"Very well," the god said. "A fate worse than death it shall be."

Revel cried out in despair, laying his head down on the cool sand. The tide was creeping closer, and he suddenly thought of Tristan, who had died this very way. Penelope would be devastated once more, and there was nothing he could do.

Poseidon bent down to speak close to Revel's ear.

"I want you to know that Despoine has a certain gift of sight," he said. "Don't worry. I'll take good care of your son."

Revel's eyes grew round in surprise. A moment later, he was gone, transported to a new and frightening world.

Part Three
Now

Chapter Eleven
The Library

Josie and Emily walked toward Main Street in fall sunshine the color of an apricot, taking care on the worn, uneven sidewalks so as not to twist an ankle. The day had warmed a little, although the girls still wore thick fleece pullovers to keep the worst of the chills at bay. Maine in October was a beautiful display, but it held a chill unlike any Josie had felt in the South. Some of it, her mom had said, was the breeze coming off the waters. A vast, dark lake lay at the end of the aunts' street and separated Bedford from Rockford, an even smaller town that was mostly just home to a couple of bars and one dilapidated old grocery store.

They had been in Bedford for two weeks and were no closer to figuring out how the two of them had managed to share a dream. Josie had tried as hard as she could to remember something about her visit to the aunts' house just before Andy disappeared, but her memories kept leading her to the library and not much else. On top of that, she and Emily had started school, enduring the curious, open stares by classmates and questions about where they were from. The other kids had mostly been polite, but Josie sensed that it was born not of kindness but rather a sense of duty shared by the community. Alice and Joan seemed to be well known and liked in their small town, and when people found out Josie and Emily were family, there was a near-palpable change in tone and body language, as though some confirmation had been given that the girls were worth talking to. It was, Josie realized, akin to a prisoner having someone with credibility vouch for him.

The changes were difficult, but there was a very cute boy in her Biology class, and that was making everything a little more tolerable. James Christopher was quiet, with dark hair and eyes. Sometimes he wore glasses, and on those days Josie had to force herself to pay attention to her teacher, lest she fail miserably and have to take Bio twice.

There hadn't been much time to explore the town, but the girls were making it a priority today. Josie was hoping something would jar her memory, and part of her was afraid it would work. Not knowing what was on the other side of those memories was eating into her sleep.

Emily just wanted to get out of the house. The aunts made her slightly nervous, although she couldn't say why, and she spent most of her time at home avoiding them. Josie had watched with growing anxiety as Emily regressed, passing the days in near-silence and retreating to her room like a ghost as soon as she could. She'd lost weight, a worry since she was already whip-thin to begin with, and the bluish circles under her eyes had darkened. To Josie, it was like watching the sun disappear behind storm clouds.

The library awaited them just ahead, creamy pillars shining gold in the afternoon light. Josie paused beneath the clock tower and took it all in, trying to place herself here on a map of time that included her brother. She vaguely recalled sitting on a bench here with Andy, counting their money. Probably before a trip to the pharmacy, a place which gurgled up in her memory as it had when they'd first arrived two weeks ago. But there were no details, so Josie took Emily's hand and led her inside.

There had been a renovation of sorts since her last visit; Josie could see that well enough without having to rely on her memories. A brand new flat-screen computer station lined one wall in the kids' section, where a giant plaster tree grew from the carpet and through the roof. It held a sturdy, low-to-the-ground treehouse that served as a reading nook for the little ones, as well as several stuffed birds along the branches. Emily immediately perked up and headed in that direction, leaving Josie behind to look at everything else.

There were few patrons there in the middle of the afternoon; one young mother was reading to a little boy of about three in a corner of the kids' area in a quiet voice, her hair pulled up into a ballerina's topknot. An older gentleman sat in a plush armchair beneath a bay window, a newspaper spread out in his lap. His head nodded over it in the warm sunshine; Josie stared for a moment at the white hairs of his beard, which seemed to glow in the light. Tiny dust motes danced around his head like fairies.

Everything seemed so…real here. Things Josie never noticed in everyday life practically sat up and sang beneath her attention, shining like coins. Even Emily seemed to feel it. Josie watched as her little sister chose a book and curled up happily in a chair shaped like a cat, looking for all the world as she had before the move to Maine. Even her blonde hair looked brighter, a luminescent halo around her fragile skull.

A sudden inspiration led Josie to the bank of computers along the wall, and she sat down in one of the comically small wooden chairs. At the old house in Kentucky, there hadn't been a desktop computer once their ancient one gave up in a spray of sparks, and the aunts didn't own one. There had never been enough money for Josie to have her own phone, something that irritated her endlessly and surely marked her as different—even more so than she already was—in the eyes of her new classmates. It hadn't occurred to her before to do some research online, but here was her chance.

Josie pulled up a search engine and typed in the year Andy had disappeared, followed by "Bedford,

Maine." There weren't many hits, which was unsurprising; most small towns don't have much in the way of newsworthy items until someone important dies or gets married. The third article down caught her eye, and she clicked on the link, bringing up a page from the local newspaper, The Bedford Sun.

"Bedford Bruiser Survives Bizarre Accident," the headline blared. She vaguely remembered seeing a sign declaring that Bedford was the home of this Bruiser, whatever or whoever that was. The date on the article was August 19, the day she and Andy had come home from the aunts' house.

Joseph Morrin, known to most Bedfordites as the Bedford Bruiser, is recovering today after a freak accident involving a mirror that might have left him paralyzed...or worse.

Morrin's wife, Sandra, says the couple was sitting in their living room watching television Friday night when a massive antique mirror hanging over the fireplace suddenly fell, showering broken glass and sharp metal splinters onto Joseph. The mirror had been in the family for generations, and the frame was carved from a single piece of black ironwood measuring over five feet long; Sandra says she estimates the mirror weighed well over 200 pounds. Joseph managed to avoid being struck by the entire piece; thanks to his athletic skills, he moved out of the way in time. The former baseball star is recovering at Bedford Memorial Hospital today with a broken arm and several stitches, something Sandra says she's profoundly grateful for.

"It could have been so much worse," she told us when we caught her at the Morrin's home on Dogwood Trace. "It was so bizarre. Short of an earthquake, I can't imagine anything strong enough to shake that mirror off the wall. Thank God Joe is still quick on his feet."

Ever the modest one, Joseph Morrin says it was just a freak accident and that he got lucky.

"That mirror has hung there for years, and I imagine that decades of slamming doors and big trucks rumbling by outside probably shook it just enough to hang there by a thread until it finally fell. It's no big deal, except now I'll have to find a way to replace a priceless heirloom," Morrin said with a grin.

Joseph Morrin broke into the world of sports at the tender age of nine years old, when his pitching arm set him apart from every other child athlete in five counties. As he moved up through the ranks on various school teams, Morrin's ability to dominate a game at any position drew the interest of several coaches who recognized his amazing potential; by his junior year of high school, he was attracting major league scouts to area games. But a shoulder injury at just seventeen years old put a hold on any aspirations Morrin had of becoming a professional ballplayer; after that, he once said, his heart wasn't in it.

Josie bit her thumb in concentration, looking at the photos that accompanied the article. One was of Morrin in the hospital, looking more cheerful than he had any right to be with his arm in a hard cast. His wife stood beside the bed with one hand on Joseph's shoulder, smiling through tears for the camera. Vase after vase of flowers filled the room, proving the reporter right; this guy was a small town hero, alright.

The second photo was of the Morrin's living room, and it was of much less quality than the first; obviously, either Joseph or his wife had taken it just after the accident. The image showed the mirror in a million pieces on the floor, with glass flung as far as the front foyer. Large slivers of wood lay strewn across the glass, looking for all the world as though an earthquake had just occurred. The entire scene gave Josie such a strong case of deja vu that she felt sick to her stomach for a moment and closed her eyes against the glare of the computer screen.

With her eyes closed, a word floated up behind them. Millieu? That was close, but still not right. It was like taking a taste of something cooking on the stove and knowing it needed a little something, but not knowing what.

"Jo?"

Josie looked up to see Emily standing near, her eyes sparkling the way they only did when she was really happy. "Hey, are you done reading already?"

Emily smiled and rolled her eyes. "Yes, I'm done already. You've been sitting here mooning over that computer for like an hour. I finished the book I was reading and started another one."

"What?" Josie laughed. "It can't have been an hour already."

But it had been. She could see that just from the way the light had changed in the room; the sun was nearly set, leaving a pink stripe at the horizon outside the big bay window. How had time gotten away from her so quickly? She watched Emily skip to the checkout desk, full of energy, hair bouncing off her shoulders, and had the strangest feeling that the library was much more than it appeared to be.

"I'm sorry, love, you'll have to bring your mom or dad in to help you get a library card," the lady at the desk was telling Emily. "But I'll tell you what. I'll give you the application and you can fill it out together at home. Would that be okay?"

"Sure!" Emily said, unfazed.

"Are you her big sister?" the woman asked Josie, her dark eyes dancing.

"Yeah, we just moved here," Josie offered. She wasn't sure why, but the woman reminded her of someone. Once again, her memory came up short, but she wondered if there was an old babysitter somewhere in her past with those same eyes. She was forever drawing a woman in her sketchbook with dark features and pale skin, her eyes as haunted as the ones you sometimes see in old Victorian portraits.

"Well, you two feel free to come in as much as you like and keep me company. Most nights it's just me and Mr. Goodman over there, and he's not much for conversation."

She nodded to the man who had fallen asleep over his newspaper, the last patron inside the library besides them. Emily giggled and took the library card application the woman was holding in one outstretched hand. The nametag on her rainbow-striped sweater read Mary.

"Thanks, we will," Josie said. "I'll have our mom fill this out."

"Excellent!" Mary said with a smile and leaned over the counter conspiratorially. "Don't worry about those kids in your class. Soon you won't be the new girl anymore, and they'll all find something else to focus on."

Josie tilted her head, studying the woman. "How did you know…?"

Mary laughed. "It's hard to be the new kid in a small town, everyone knows that. But you're always welcome here."

"Thanks," Josie said with a little frown. She had never been a fan of strangers who felt they had her figured out; there had been enough of that back home, right after Andy had disappeared.

With the library card application carefully folded and tucked away in her pocket, Josie led Emily to the front doors, looking back over her shoulder as she did so. Everything seemed normal at first glance, but there was something about the light that made her uneasy, only because it was unnaturally perfect. Like much of the town, it seemed like a movie set.

Chapter Twelve
The Prophecy

"M'lord?"

Shadow opened his eyes to the ceiling, feeling the unwelcome sensation of pins and needles in his legs as he moved them down from his desk. He had taken to meditating every day, trying to focus and harness his energy to find the power he knew still dwelled within him. It was of no use. Poseidon had stripped everything from him. He had been thorough.

As for the boy, he had been useless. Shadow had threatened him, chained him to a chair and questioned him mercilessly for three days while one of his guards stood by with a whip; when he didn't comply, the boy was rewarded with a snap to the back. He'd taken sixteen lashes and was brutally bloodied, but still insisted he didn't know where the mirror was. Shadow had finally let him go, tired of the theatrics. He'd searched the rubble after the tunnel's collapse, he had searched the bodies of Annika and Rolo himself, just to make sure.

The only path left was the boy's sister, but he had no way of getting to her now. The faceless spirits had retreated to the woods surrounding the In Between to find sustenance, something they did every so often and which Shadow did not completely understand.

If he were to be honest with himself, he would have to admit that he was frightened by the spirits, a fear made all the more real by the fact that he had no control over them. They were here long before he himself had arrived, and would likely be around long after he was gone. He would have to be patient and wait until they came back before he carried out a new plan, whatever it may be. Besides, if the girl had the mirror, it stood to reason that she would have used it to find her brother by now.

"What is it?" he called now, wearier than he had ever been.

Rowan Murphy stood in the doorway, draped in a cloak the color of a storm. He had been keeping his distance from Shadow recently, ever since the debacle with the children, because he felt partly responsible. As Shadow's right-hand man, it was Rowan's responsibility to know the ins and outs of the castle, the grounds, the movements of the villagers. He had been called away just before the incident to visit his ailing mother and was forced to stay and make preparations for her to be laid to rest; otherwise, had would have been in the castle that day. To know that these children, these interlopers, had somehow infiltrated their world and had stolen something valuable from Shadow was almost inconceivable, and had Shadow been a lesser being he might have had Rowan's head for allowing it to happen under his nose. Yet his head—and his life—had been spared, and Rowan was all the more grateful to him. Ever the faithful servant, he had seen that the tunnels were cleaned up and repaired immediately and that the bodies of Rolo and Annika were buried in a simple ceremony. Now began the long road of earning back Shadow's trust.

"Master Killian is here, sir. He's waiting in the solarium."

Shadow sat up fully and rubbed the back of his neck, wishing he could have a few more moments to himself but aware that this meeting was a long time coming. He'd been trying to speak with Killian for many returns of the sun about everything that had happened, in part because Killian was the most revered man in the In Between; at 103 years old, he was still as mentally agile as a man in his twenties, and he was not only wise but extremely fair and kind. Shadow looked up to him, in his way, although he knew he couldn't rule this land with such a gentle hand. It was no way to get things done in a place where time meant nothing, and the people were rejects from their own countries.

Of course, Killian was also a very skilled prophet, which made him invaluable to Shadow.

"Revel," Killian said as he entered. He was no more than five-and-a-half feet tall, but he seemed to fill the room as he swept in, something Shadow envied more than he would like to admit. "So good to see you again."

"It's been too long," Shadow agreed, taking Killian's forearm in greeting. "I trust Rowan took good care of you?"

"Oh, yes. Such a fine young man. He always remembers that I much prefer black Chai tea to Oolong."

"I am sorry to have kept you waiting. I've been pondering this problem I have, and I became a little lost in my thoughts."

"Tell me," Killian said, taking a seat.

Shadow unraveled his story slowly, beginning with the open portal and moving on to the children and fantastical mirror, which had allowed him to travel once again. When he got to the part about his return—and the subsequent violence resulting in the loss of the mirror—Killian held up a hand.

"Say no more," he said. Killian preferred not to know too much about the details of Shadow's life so that he could more accurately predict what was coming. "I have been meditating of late, sometimes from mealtime to mealtime. Today, I paid a visit to the old citadel."

"But there's nothing there anymore. Just ash and rubble."

Killian smiled and looked out the window, toward the horizon, as though he hadn't heard Shadow. "When I was a younger man, I used to climb Mt. Orion often and sift through the remains of that place. It was the original home of Detrus and Grimble, did you know that? They guarded the entire realm once upon a time before it was a cursed place."

Shadow shook his head minutely, humbled to learn something new about the In Between. His gargoyles rarely spoke of the past in any detail, even when pressed, so Shadow had given up a long time ago.

"There is a spot on the mountain, well hidden in a grave of ash, that was once a meeting place for the greatest minds in the land. The largest room in the citadel was made of marble and onyx, and even on the hottest of days it kept us cool." Killian paused and stroked his long, silvery beard for a moment in reflection. "When the citadel fell, that room collapsed into an underground vault below. It had been a place to go in the event of an attack, and only those in the highest ranks knew about it. Suddenly, I realized why that room stayed cool always."

"And the vault is still there?"

Killian nodded slowly. "Indeed, it is. Buried beneath the detritus and dust, there lies a room that once held all the weapons in the In Between, both magical and not. We never thought we would actually go to war, not with Poseidon and his people, but everyone wanted to be prepared. If I recall, there was a Gatling gun there taken from the

American Civil War that still worked. The vault is empty now, of course—the raiders came and stripped it soon after Poseidon took his leave—but sometimes, even among the ash, one can find a treasure. For me, it was the memory of a vision I had long ago."

Killian rummaged inside his cloak for a moment and brought out a small, ravaged piece of paper. It was obviously very old, as it was nothing more than a thin scrap through which Shadow could see the light filtering, and Killian was holding it so reverently he knew it was something special.

"This parchment was used only for the most high-level documents. If you look closely, you can see the fine gold filaments that the king insisted be placed inside all his correspondence. This was from a letter he'd written to me requesting my presence at the last meeting he ever had, and on that afternoon I wrote upon it a prophecy I still to this day don't understand. I don't know if one has anything to do with the other, but after I had the vision, I felt so fatigued I sent word back to the king to let him know I wouldn't be able to attend the meeting. Two hours later, everyone at the citadel was dead, and I was left with this message from the future, a meaningless collection of letters that has nagged at my brain. Until now."

"And the vision?" Shadow asked.

"A word, I suppose, although I can't make heads or tails of it."

Killian leaned forward with the slip of paper between his fingers so that Shadow could take it, but for the briefest of moments, he hesitated. This was either the answer to his problem that had just fallen into his lap, or it was a glimpse into a catastrophic future. Perhaps both.

"Tell me what you think it means," he said finally, taking the paper from Killian. Written upon it, in a shaky, old fashioned script, were the letters E M B U R.

"I can't even begin to guess," Killian said sadly. "I wish I could be of more help. But I can tell you this: I had a dream during my last sleep in which fire and water met, and the words on this piece of paper floated up in my mind. I had forgotten about it, thought it was long gone, but when I searched my books there, it was, stuck between the pages of my favorite text. I believe it has something to do with Poseidon. If you find EMBUR, you'll find your answer."

"You think this EMBUR is connected to the mirror? That it could help me travel once again?"

"That I do not know," Killian said. "But I think the dream was a warning. I believe we are on the precipice of a war, Revel. A great war in which many souls will be taken. My advice to you is to attune your focus."

Shadow stood, folded his hands behind his back, and walked slowly to the great floor-to-ceiling window which gave him a bird's-eye view of the land. His land. His thoughts turned to that day in the tunnels, to where he'd gone with the help of the mirror, and a small ache began to work its way through his chest.

"You're aware of how long I've waited to travel to the World?" he asked with his back turned. "I've been here so long that I myself do not know how old I am. After all this time, to have found a way to journey again only to have it snatched away from mw…it's torture. It is torture, plain and simple."

He turned to Killian. "If you do not know what the prophecy means, it is tantamount to looking for a needle in a haystack. The boy is here now, and he will help me open the portal. He has magic in him, I can smell it. I'll use him to cross through and travel. To look for this EMBUR. To find…" He trailed off, setting his jaw.

Killian smiled sadly and shook his head. "I understand that you loved her—"

"I still love her!" Shadow screamed, his voice cracking with emotion. "Every breath without her is like a knife in my chest. You'll never…you can't understand that."

With great effort, Killian stood and made his way to the window, placing a gentle hand on Shadow's arm. "I understand more than you think, my boy. But I am concerned that these thoughts of what might have been are taking you away from the real problem at hand, and that even if you find a key that will allow you to travel once more, you will forget one very important thing."

"What's that?" Shadow asked raggedly.

"Time is different here," Killian said. "If you travel beyond the boundaries of the In Between without this mirror, your body will very likely begin to age rapidly, and you will die."

Shadow looked out the window once more, at the land under his survey. Beneath purple clouds, people were hurrying back and forth, trying to finish their chores before the impending storm cracked open the sky.

"Then I'll just have to ask for help in finding it," said Shadow. "I'm sure the good people of the In Between will be more than happy to assist me."

Killian stroked his beard thoughtfully. "What exactly did you see when you traveled that day, my boy?"

"Everything," Shadow said in a low tone. "The World."

∞

Behind the bookcase in the solarium, concealed by a thick layer of stone, Andy stood listening. Their words were muffled, but he had definitely heard the words "key," "travel," and "mirror."

Since his return, he had made it his mission to find all the tunnels in the In Between, in part because he felt it was what Annika would have wanted, and his debt to her memory was large. With the help of Alek, he'd come a long way. Beneath the castle, there was a huge webwork of passageways, so big that he doubted even the Shadow Man knew about some of them, the ones that were filled with sharp rocks or were so small that even Andy—who was painfully thin—had a hard time getting through them. They were a way for him to pass the hours—whatever that meant in this forsaken land —but they also allowed him to stay close to the Shadow Man, to keep an ear to the ground, so to speak, and learn what his plans were. He was young, but he was far from stupid; survival was the name of the game in the In Between, and that meant being careful.

Shadow had let Andy go, in his way; he'd grown too impatient to continue his harassment after Andy had taken so many lashes without giving up any information. But that didn't mean Andy was free.

In the days that followed his punishment, Andy had lived a half-life, subsisting on the food that Alek and a few of his other friends could spare and sleeping on a scratchy mat of straw on the floor of Annika's hut. It hadn't seemed right to take her bed, even though the floor was hard-packed dirt. Shadow had men working for him as his eyes and ears throughout the In Between, and although Andy thought he could spot them easily by now, it wasn't worth the risk to try to build his own hut or share in the crops. Shadow had made it clear that he was allowing Andy to leave the castle with his life and nothing else. Those were the terms for a so-called thief, which were tantamount to a death sentence. Surviving in the In Between on the wrong side of the Shadow Man was near impossible, Andy had learned.

Now, as he listened to Shadow and the old man speak of prophecies and keys, he felt something bubbling up inside him. It felt like a golden ball of light sitting in his chest, just beneath his ribcage, something that could not be contained. It was an idea and a feeling at once, the realization that this was bigger than him. He pictured the brass key Josie had found during one of their first trips here, the one with the little purple stone. It must be the one they were talking about, but what had she done with it? Would she even still have it?

Andy could feel the desperation that had sat so heavily on his shoulders begin to lighten as a plan formed in his mind. He turned an object over and over in his hands and closed his eyes, an object Alek had given to him just minutes before he had entered the tunnels.

"I was called upon to help pull apart the rubble and find Rolo and...Annika," Alek had said. Andy only nodded and lowered his head, ashamed that he had not attended the funeral for his friend. There were too many pairs of eyes there, keeping watch for Shadow; there was too much guilt in his heart. "I found this."

Alek had handed him a small parcel wrapped in linen, and when he took it in his hands, he knew immediately what it was. His stomach jumped into his throat, and he tore at the wrapping with shaking fingers, hardly able to believe his good fortune. He stared down at the item inside, eyes filling with tears when he realized what it meant.

"The mirror," he said.

"It must have shattered in the fight," Alek said sadly. "I found it half-buried in the weeds just outside the entrance Annika used to sneak you back into the castle that day. I reckon it got thrown outside when the tunnels collapsed. Shadow had all his men searching the debris for it, but I thought you should have it."

Andy handled it now, twisting it gently in his hands, careful not to cut himself on one of the jagged pieces. He had tried over and over to get it to work, to allow him to travel once more, but whatever magic was inside it had fled. Looking at the dull surface of the glass, a nagging thought came to him, one that had kept him awake nights since it had first popped into his mind. How had he and Josie gotten away that day without the mirror? In the initial terror of their escape, the idea hadn't occurred to him, and once they got home, his memories had begun to trickle away from him. It wasn't until recently that he realized what had happened.

He could no longer continue this existence, this meager life that kept him slinking around a doomed land with a scarred back, waiting like an old dog to be kicked again. He had to get out of the village and find a way to fix the mirror. He had to get to Josie, find the key, and save his family from Shadow Man's wrath.

Chapter Thirteen
Halloween

On Halloween, Josie awoke in a good mood. It had always been one of her favorite holidays, even though she didn't get the day off from school and she was too old to trick-or-treat. For the past few years, she'd taken Emily on the rounds, and after they came home with a sack full of loot, they'd make pumpkin-shaped sugar cookies with their mom and decorate them with gooey orange icing before settling in to watch a spooky movie.

Although this year would be a little different, Josie was still looking forward to it. The aunts had decorated the entire house with black and orange crepe-paper, old-fashioned cutouts of skeleton faces and Frankenstein's monster heads, and gauzy mummies that hung from the light fixtures. Aunt Joan had coaxed Emily into helping her make those out of cheesecloth, and it had prompted one of the few genuine smiles from her little sister since the move.

Josie herself had put her artistic talent to good use and created little tableaus around the house: an old silver platter that held stacked paper-mache skulls, a stuffed crow, and graveyard moss for the mantel in the formal living room; apothecary jars filled with Halloween candy across the top of the kitchen cabinets; an antique mirror with a gold frame that held a carefully-placed silver etching Josie had done of a young Victorian girl, modeled after the face she was always drawing in her sketchbook. When she hung the mirror in the foyer, it looked as though the girl was trapped inside, screaming at Josie to let her out. The effect was so unsettling that she ended up moving the mirror to the mudroom, where she didn't have to cross in front of it every day.

When she arrived at school, there were dancing skeletons hanging from every other locker, and the mood was festive. Lots of kids had come in costume, something that was heartily encouraged by the school board since there was no money for a dance this year. Josie suspected that had something to do with the new football uniforms, but didn't mention it; she had enough to worry about without alienating her classmates.

She herself had chosen a flowy, shimmery blue dress with a Grecian-inspired bust, and a gold armlet that encircled her right bicep. She'd been up early braiding her hair so that it hung in a long plait down her back, and her mom had helped her twine gold ribbon through it. She looked like an extra from *Game Of Thrones,* which was fine with her. She wasn't going for a character; she wanted to create her own. The dress had been a lucky find at a thrift store back home; she'd worn it last year for Halloween, and it was only a little tighter now. She found herself standing and sitting a little straighter than she usually did because of the fit, something which had given her a curious boost of confidence when she tried it on at home.

Now that she was actually at school, the idea of a costume seemed *extremely* silly. What if no one else had dressed up? She felt herself sweating through her dress and forced herself to calm down as she approached the door to her homeroom. Compared to everything else she'd been through, this should be cake.

Still, she breathed a sigh of relief when she walked in and saw most of the class dressed up. The popular group—Devon, Kennedy, and Autumn—stood by the windows, all wearing different versions of a Harley Quinn costume. They looked gossipy, blonde heads bent towards one another conspiratorially. Two boys in "ghost killer" masks were chasing each other around the room, while several other people huddled around someone's phone to listen to a new song by DJ AKorn. Josie's friends, Alexa Chang and Mike Noble, sat in the back, watching all the action with amusement. It always took Mr. Bierman a while to get to homeroom because he was in charge of arranging the morning announcements, so they had a few minutes to talk.

"Heyyy," Alexa said as Josie approached. "Look at you, Miss Girl! Killer dress, where'd you get it?"

"Back home," Josie said with a smile. "It's actually last year's. I didn't really have time to put together something new."

"Looks good," Mike said appreciatively, and Josie felt her cheeks warm. It was nice to be noticed, but she'd rather it came from someone else...

She looked around the room and spotted James on the far side, near the Blonde Squad, eating what looked like sour taffy and reading a Neil Gaiman comic. *The Sandman* was written across the front; the artwork was beautiful. Josie made a mental note to check it out while marveling at how cool James seemed to be at all times. He didn't belong to a crowd, didn't care what everyone else was doing. She wished she could be that nonchalant when it came to school.

"Good morning everyone," Mr. Bierman said dryly from the doorway.

The chaos became a hushed flurry of action as twenty students rushed to their desks.

"I see you're all full of the Halloween 'spirit,'" Mr. Bierman quipped, laughing at his own joke. He had a coffee stain on his tie already.

"Weak," Alexa whispered from behind Josie.

"Class, I'd like to introduce you to...where did she run off to? Oh here she is," Mr. Bierman said, gesturing towards the open door. A girl stood there, looking for all the world like she'd rather be sitting in a dentist's chair than where she was. Tall and exquisitely pretty, with dark, gleaming skin and almond-shaped eyes, she wore a multitude of brightly-colored beaded bracelets stacked on both forearms almost up to her elbows, a printed pillowcase dress that circled her neck and exposed her shoulder blades, and tall leather gladiator sandals that nearly reached her knees. Her hair was in a soft, natural afro that surrounded her head like a halo.

"Class, this is Shanti Xavier. She's joining us for the rest of the school year from New Haven, so give her a nice welcome," Mr. Bierman said before turning on the television for the morning announcements. There was a smattering of weak applause from the class as Shanti made her way through the room to an empty desk directly across from Josie.

As she passed the Blonde Squad, Devon whispered, "Nice costume," drawing snickers from her lackeys. Shanti stopped in her tracks, looking down regally at Devon.

"I'm not wearing a costume."

The blondes laughed in disbelief as Shanti walked to her desk and sat down. Josie could feel herself staring at this confident girl in awe.

"I'm Josie," she said softly. "I'm new here, too. Don't worry about those girls. They're miserable, so they spread it around."

"I'm not worried about them," Shanti said with a little smile, and turned her attention to the television.

"Wow," Alexa whispered.

"Yeah," Josie whispered back.

∞

When Josie and Emily arrived at home after school, they were greeted with the scents of homemade donuts and hot apple cider. The entire house smelled like fall, and Josie breathed deep. Heavenly.

The aunts were waiting for them in the kitchen; Alice was ladling cider into small Mason jars which had been tied with orange raffia, and Joan was drizzling icing onto a stack of donuts sitting on a tarnished silver platter. The temperature had dropped outside, and rain clouds had swooped in, making the kitchen appear even brighter and more cheery than usual.

"Happy Halloween!" Alice cried, handing each of the girls their own jar of cider. "There's nothing better on a chilly fall day than something to warm you up. Oh! Wait!"

She grabbed a couple of cinnamon sticks from a ceramic jug on the counter and plopped one into each glass, making Em giggle. "Can't forget the cinnamon!"

"This is awesome," Josie said, gratefully taking a donut from Aunt Joan. It was still warm and was thick with sugary icing. "Halloween is the best."

"We agree," Joan said with a little wink. She whipped off her apron and reached beneath the counter, taking a large witch's hat from the shelf and placing it stylishly on her head. Her costume had been hidden, but now the girls could see the full effect: a shimmery black gown with black lace sleeves and a velvet choker set with a purple stone. The peaked hat was the perfect final touch; she looked like a real Victorian witch, complete with black pointy-toed boots.

"Oh my gosh!" Emily said brightly. "You look so cool!"

"The best seal of approval any aunt could hope for," Joan said, hugging Emily.

"I'd better go get ready," Alice said, putting her own apron away. "Just wait until you see *my* costume. I did way better than a boring old witch."

"Just for that I'm not saving you any of these donuts," Joan said, taking a hearty bite from one.

"I've already had more than my legal limit," Alice said with a laugh as she went upstairs.

Josie sat on one of the stools at the counter while Emily took her backpack upstairs. "This is really nice," she said, gesturing to the decorations and food. "We've always loved Halloween."

"We have, too. I thought it would be fun to have the house nice and festive for you girls."

"Alice seems...really happy," Josie said carefully. She didn't quite know how to word her observation that her aunt seemed more sane than usual.

"Oh, this time of year is her favorite. She's been very lucid today. I think it's good for her to have something to do, and baking always calms her nerves," Joan said with a smile. "Are you going trick-or-treating later?"

"I'll take Emily around. I think I've officially aged out of that activity."

"Nonsense! You're never too old to trick-or-treat! Well, maybe once you hit 60, you should reconsider. But 14? Pish."

Josie laughed. "Noted. Hey, where's my mom?"

"She said she'd be working tonight."

Josie put down her donut. "She got a job?"

"At a real estate firm," Joan said, piling dirty dishes in the sink. "She didn't give me any details. Perhaps she didn't want to jinx it. She seemed to be in a hurry, so I didn't press her."

"Well, that's great," Josie said, and she meant it...but it still stung not to be included in her mom's plans.

∞

Josie waited up for her mom after Emily went to bed. Trick-or-treat had been amazing but tiring, and her little sister was snoring from her bed when

Josie walked by, still wearing most of her Cruella de Vil costume.

"Hey, kiddo," Elizabeth said as she walked into the living room. She dumped her bag into a chair and sat beside Josie on the couch. "How was trick-or-treat?"

"It was fine."

"Did you get any pictures of Emily in her costume? I didn't get to see it all put together."

"Yeah."

Elizabeth nudged her gently with an elbow. "Hey. What's wrong?"

Josie sighed. "Nothing, except I've been wondering why my mother didn't tell me she got a job."

"Ah. Joan told you."

"She did," Josie said. "Why didn't you?"

Elizabeth leaned back and kicked her shoes off. "I don't know, Jo. Maybe because I knew it would be this huge thing for us, and I would feel pressure to make it work. I already feel pressure."

"From me?"

"No, babe. Not at all. Just from myself, from wanting to be the best mother I can be to my girls all on my own. It's not easy to do the work of both parents."

"We know that, Mom. We don't expect you to be perfect, but there's no way we can make things work if we start keeping secrets."

Elizabeth smiled. "When did you get so wise?"

"I watch a lot of BBC shows," Josie deadpanned.

Chapter Fourteen
Secrets, Secrets

Andy sat quietly in the back of a very crowded room, watching anxiously as the noise level grew louder and louder. Emotions were high, but that was to be expected; rumors had been running wild about the Shadow Man and his search for the mirror, and although Andy didn't understand all of it and didn't want to, he knew this could be a turning point in his life within the boundaries of the In Between.

Alek stood at the front of the room, holding his hands up to indicate the need for quiet. If news spread to Shadow that there was a meeting of any kind going on, there would be repercussions. He had allowed them all to exist in his land for reasons known only to him, but there was a general consensus that he would not tolerate even a whiff of rebellion, and where would that leave them all? Andy shuddered to think.

There was a small group of villagers acting as lookouts, hiding in strategic locations around the hut where Alek's brother Tomas made his home. It was set away from the rest of the village, nearly a mile outside of the circle of huts where most of them lived, and backed up to the cliffs that over-looked The Pits. That meant it was only exposed on three sides, and the lookouts were well-trained to spot intruders. They were relatively safe here, but it paid to take precautions.

"Listen," Alek was saying now. The voices in the room became hushed murmurs, a sound that re-minded Andy of rushing bees. The heat of the hut was beginning to make him drowsy, and he was having a hard time following the thread of the conversation, but he knew what everyone was wor-ried about: the fact that Shadow was actively look-ing for the mirror meant he could possibly gain the ability to travel between worlds again soon. He was so unpredictable that no one wanted to think about the changes that would bring to the In Be-tween. It could be a difficult, ugly place to live at times, but it was all they had. Andy felt a flash of guilt as he thought of his own family waiting for him to return. Most of the residents had given up hope of being reunited with their loved ones long ago.

"I think it's important not to get overwhelmed just yet," Alek said. "We don't have many facts, but I can tell you that my brother and I have both overheard Shadow talking about this mirror and how badly he wants it. There's not a doubt in ei-ther of our minds that if he finds it, he'll start traveling again. What that means for us is up for debate, but I think we can all agree that it's important—at least in the short term—to make sure he doesn't get his hands on it. If anyone finds it, I think it should be brought to this group immediately so we can keep it safe."

Andy had been watching Alek intently, and now his friend's eyes flicked briefly to his before moving across the rest of the room.

"What gives you the right to decide?" asked a girl called Kyra. Andy recalled that she had a little brother named Ryan and spotted him sitting at the back of the room, listening intently. Seeing the two of them reminded him of his own relationship with Josie and he looked down at his hands.

"Yeah, who says the mirror wouldn't be a good thing for all of us?" echoed her friend, an older girl with frizzy red hair whose name Andy couldn't remember. "Why can't we make a pact to figure out how to use it for ourselves? This could be our way home!"

At that, the noise level quickly grew to a roar again, and Andy felt anxiety gnaw at his stomach. *If only they knew the truth*, he thought.

"Guys, guys!" Tomas yelled, standing beside his brother. He had to cup his hands around his mouth to make himself heard. "First of all, there's no proof that we could figure out how to work this mirror even if we did find it."

"Second of all," Alek said once the room had calmed down a bit, "We may have numbers, but none of us is a match for Shadow or his men. Some of us who have been here since the beginning have seen his work. Annika saw it up close."

There were nods of agreement around the room at that.

"Look, we all want to go home," Alek said. "But the truth is, even if we did find the mirror, and even if we could make it work...none of us knows what happens to people who travel back from the In Between without a portal. Time is too unpredictable here, and there's no way to tell how long we've been gone. Some of us who have been here the longest...our families have probably stopped looking for us."

Here, he choked up, and Andy felt himself doing the same. It was a thought that had crossed his mind a hundred times since he'd been here. Across the room, the sound of sniffles rippled like a soft wave.

"I don't accept this," Kyra said angrily, standing up. "I'm going to look for that mirror, and if I find it, I'm going home. You can come with me or you can stay here and rot with that madman."

And then something happened that Andy had sensed building up and was dreading: as she turned to leave, several others stood and followed her. They filed out, shuffling their feet, some with looks of confused anger on their faces. After a few moments, only about half of the original group remained seated.

Alek sighed tiredly. "I'm not trying to tell anyone what they should or shouldn't do. I just want us to be smart about this."

Andy stood up. "I'm with you."

"Me, too," said a short boy with a small gold stud in his left ear.

There were several echoes of the same sentiment across the room for a moment, and Alek smiled.

"Alright, then. If anyone finds anything resembling a mirror, bring it to me and we'll figure out what to do next. Until then, I think we should lie low."

The group dispersed slowly, talking amongst themselves. Andy moved to stand with Alek and Tomas, running a hand nervously through his hair as he did so.

"What are we going to do?" he asked shakily. "I don't want to be the keeper of this thing anymore. I think one of you should hold on to it."

Alek shook his head. "I think it's meant to be with you. I don't know why. It's just something I feel."

"Can't we just tell them you found it and that it's broken? That would put an end to this."

"We could, but it might only create more problems," Tomas said. "If Shadow finds out the mirror is here, he'll obliterate us for hiding it from him. I think this is the best plan. Just hold on to it for a little while longer. We need to think."

Andy sighed. "Okay. But I want to be in on whatever plan you come up with. I have to get home."

"We all do," Alek said quietly.

"I know," Andy said, hanging his head. "And I'm sorry that I never thanked you properly for saving us. I know Annika would want me to thank you, too."

Alek shook his head minutely. "What do you mean?"

"You were in the tunnels that day, you handed her the river water to throw at Rolo. Without that poison, we never would have gotten away. I may be stuck here again, but at least my sister got away."

Alek frowned. "I didn't give Annika any river water."

"But...I saw her take the vial from someone. I couldn't see who it was, but I assumed it was you because you'd just been there with us."

Alek shook his head again. "As soon as the three of you were near the portal, I ran out to find Tomas so we could try to intercept Shadow's men. I was nowhere near the tunnels when they collapsed."

∞

Time flowed on, much like the Salacia River. As always, the sun and moon traded places either far too quickly or far too slowly; it seemed they acted of their own volition here and didn't abide by the laws of astrophysics. It was impossible to create even a rudimentary calendar, but Andy got the sense that the meeting hadn't been that long ago. Days, perhaps. But things were moving with frightening speed in the village.

Kyra had taken the position of leader to the group that had followed her out; no one challenged this decision, and to Andy, it felt like a sea-change, like the first step toward a battle. Sides had been drawn; this group did not mingle with the others, but kept to themselves and held brief meetings late at night. They never met in the same place twice; they weren't stupid. Twice Andy had been on the verge of asking Alek whether they should send in a spy to try to find out what the meetings were about, and twice he stopped himself. It wouldn't do to get caught up in these village politics, especially when the object everyone was so concerned about was useless at the moment. Safe, but useless.

When the sun was a blood orange on the horizon, Andy went to Alek's place to scrounge some dinner and talk about Shadow. He hadn't forgotten about the mysterious poison provider; it nibbled at the edge of his brain like an itch he couldn't scratch. However, more important things were front and center at the moment, and he thought that if he could understand who Shadow was and why he had come to be here, he might figure out a way to get home. He had told Alek about what he'd heard while hiding behind the bookcase; now he wanted some answers.

"No one knows for sure, but I've heard some stories," Alek said, chewing on a piece of straw as he chopped carrots, turnips, and onions for a stew. Outside the window, twilight was trickling down, mixing purple with orange like watercolors on a tray.

"What kind of stories?"

"Well, when Tomas and I first came here, Detrus and Grimble hated each other. They used to argue day and night, and it drove Shadow mad. Eventually, he told them if they didn't stop he'd move them to The Pits, and that shut them up. But before he did, Tomas overheard them talking about the In Between and how it came to be. Don't eat those raw, you'll be on the pot forever," Alek said, slapping Andy's hand away from the purple carrots he had just chopped.

"So what were they saying?"

"A load of nonsense, mostly. Something about a curse, though, which piqued Tomas' interest. They were talking about Poseidon and a girl…Tomas got the feeling she was Poseidon's daughter. Shadow was in love with her, and they ran off together, and her pop didn't like that. He stripped ol' Shadow of his powers, banished him here, and the rest is history."

"Poseidon…the sea god?"

"The one and only," Alek said, tasting the broth with a grimace. "Needs more salt."

It had never occurred to Andy that there were other magical beings outside of this realm, that there could potentially be other universes where time didn't work properly. What if there were people trapped there as they were here? He thought of all the posters he'd seen back in the real world for missing people and shuddered.

"So what is this place? Something Poseidon concocted as a punishment?"

"Could be, but I don't think he would have made all those portals if he wanted Shadow to live the rest of his days alone. Besides, there are remains up on Orion from a civilization that lived long before we came here. People say there was a war, that Poseidon swooped in and took everything with his army, and it makes sense. Personally, I think this is just a place that was handy for him. Like a dumping ground. Secluded after he'd taken everything he wanted, warped; no one would have found Shadow if they hadn't stumbled into one of those portals. I don't think Poseidon knows about those at all."

"So…if we find this girl he was in love with, maybe she'll get her dad to lift the curse."

"I don't think it's that easy," Alek said, laughing. "I don't even know if she's still alive."

"Yeah," Andy said softly, gnawing on the edge of his thumbnail. "But it's a place to start."

"I suppose we could ask Detrus and Grimble what they know. It will be dangerous, though, getting that close to the castle. Plus, they might tell Shadow we were asking questions."

Andy thought for a moment. When he looked up, his expression was grim. "But will it be as dangerous as dividing the village? I don't want to be responsible for a war."

Alek sighed. "I don't know if we have much choice."

Chapter Fifteen
The Darkened Mirror

November 1st was ripe with damp, the kind that squishes up through your boots and makes a person long for a warm quilt.

Josie and Emily had originally planned to go to the library; their mother was at work and the aunts were busy with their book club. Setting out that morning had made the girls reconsider the library and head straight back into the house where they took refuge in Josie's warm bed with Emily's bag of Halloween candy between them.

"Who is this Bruiser person, again?" Emily asked.

"He's a baseball player."

"You don't like baseball."

"I'm not tracking him down because I'm a fan, I want to talk to him about something that happened on the day Andy disappeared."

"Do you think he knows who the Shadow Man is?" Emily asked hopefully, plucking a peanut butter cup from the top of the loot bag.

"I doubt it, but I think something important happened here that day. Do you remember how I told you I can't really remember much about our trips here?"

"Yeah?"

"Well, I found a picture of this guy's house when we were at the library, and I think I almost remembered something. It's going to drive me nuts if I don't figure it out." She looked down at Em, who was wearing a doubtful expression. "I know it sounds crazy. But I have to try."

"I'm scared," Emily said. "I'm tired, and I think I'm having nightmares every night that I can't remember and I'm scared."

"Hey," Josie said softly, pushing aside the candy bag to move closer to her sister. "It's gonna be okay. I don't know what's going on, but I'm going to do my best to figure it out. And if I can't, and things are still feeling weird by Christmas, I'll tell Mom we need to move. She has a job now, she should be able to save up some money by then for an apartment."

Emily sniffed. "Really?"

"Promise," Josie said, holding out her pinkie. Emily locked hers around it in the age-old gesture of sibling-promises everywhere and nodded.

"Okay."

"Listen, I want to go see this Bruiser guy. He just lives a few minutes from here. You wanna come with? The aunts will be home soon if you want to stay here."

"I'm not staying in this creepy place by myself," Emily said, hopping off the bed to put her shoes on.

"You sure? I bet the ghosts won't mind. They don't come out until after midnight anyway—"

"Stop."

"And by that time you're already asleep and vulnerable in your bed—"

"Stop it."

"In the dark, alone—"

"Josie, shut up!"

∞

The Morrin home was well-tended, with a neat front lawn and windows that sparkled in the afternoon sun. Josie knocked on the door with a knot in her belly, rehearsing inwardly what she intended to say. Even with preparation, she felt like she was standing at the edge of a cliff, about to throw herself into the wind. Something felt off in this town, and though she had sensed it briefly at the library, it was much stronger here: a vibration, almost, a difference in air quality that left her heart beating too hard.

Sandra Morrin opened the door with an expectant smile, perhaps waiting for a sales pitch about a school fundraiser. Josie tried to look normal even as her blood galloped in her veins. "Yes?"

"Hi, Mrs. Morrin. I'm sorry to show up unannounced, but I was wondering if we could come in and talk to you and Mr. Morrin about the night he was injured?"

Sandra's smile faltered the tiniest bit. "What for?"

"It's sort of complicated."

"I don't know…" Mrs. Morrin began."For heaven's sake, honey, let them in," Joseph Morrin said from behind her. He was a big man, imposing, but he had kind eyes, and Josie was immediately put at ease. "I don't know what's on your mind, but I'm happy to try to help."

"Thank you," Josie said, relieved. Emily followed her inside, where a spacious living room awaited them. The girls took a seat beside one another on the plush couch and waited for the Morrins to settle into matching recliners.

"Would you like something to drink? I have some iced tea," Mrs. Morrin said.

"Oh, no, thank you," said Josie. "We're sorry to bother you, and we won't stay long. I was just wondering if you could tell us anything you remember about the night of your accident. Specifically, if you remember anything odd happening in the neighborhood around that time."

Joseph and Sandra looked at one another, puzzled.

"Well, no, I don't recall anything out of the ordinary other than the mirror falling," Joseph said. "It was a normal evening, the street was quiet as always. We were watching the news when it happened, I believe, although I couldn't tell you what the report was about."

"Can I ask how you heard about the accident?" Sandra asked Josie.

"I read about it in the newspaper. See, our brother, Andy…he disappeared that same night. He vanished from his bedroom at our home in Kentucky, right after we'd left here. We were visiting our aunts over summer break and…" Josie trailed off.

"We were just wondering if maybe something strange was going on in the area," Emily finished for her. Josie took her sister's hand gratefully.

"I know it's a long shot, but we've never had any leads," Josie said. "We recently moved here with our mother, and I thought maybe…"

"Of course," Joseph said softly. "You poor dears. I'm sorry I can't be of more help, but I honestly can't think of anything out of the ordinary that night. I've been over it a million times in my mind, trying to remember if a large truck went by that might have rattled the mirror, or even if it might have been a tremor. I looked it up online, and there are no records of any seismic activity around here on that date."

"Well, thank you for talking to us," Josie said. "Like I said, we knew it was a long shot, but it just seemed like an odd coincidence."

"I wish we had some answers for you," Sandra said. "I'm so sorry you've had to go through this."

"Thank you," Emily said, and Josie was glad because she suddenly had a lump in her throat.

"Just out of curiosity," Josie said, "What did you do with the mirror frame?"

"We were able to save it," Sandra said. "It's out in the garage, would you like to see it?"

The girls followed Sandra through the kitchen and into a large two-car garage. Against the far wall leaned something huge, covered with a blue canvas tarp to protect it from dust. Even without glass, the mirror was a grand thing to behold: taller than Emily and longer than either girl. The frame was dark wood, exquisitely carved, full of history. The sisters stepped back to better appreciate the full effect as Sandra finished pulling away the tarp.

"Wow," Emily said.

"I agree," said Josie. "I can't believe Mr. Morrin wasn't hurt worse than he was!"

"He was very fortunate," Sandra said with a nod. "I couldn't bear to get rid of it, but I'm not sure we'll ever put glass into it again. It's just too heavy."

A faint beeping sound began from inside the house, and Sandra smiled apologetically. "Let me just go take those cookies out of the oven. Stay out here as long as you like!"

The girls stood silent for a moment, looking at the mirror frame. After a moment, Josie stepped forward and touched it with a frown. "Do you remember what Aunt Alice said on our first day here? In the kitchen…something about a mirror?"

Emily nodded. "She said, 'You can find them in the back of the mirror.'"

"That's right," Josie said softly. "I think Aunt Alice knows a few things we don't."

"About Andy?"

Josie shook her head. "Not directly about him, I don't think…but it has to be more than a coincidence. We should talk to her. I keep almost remembering things about our last summer here. It's like having a word on the tip of your tongue but you can't find it." Suddenly Josie stopped and turned, facing the door to the house. "Do you smell that?"

"The cookies?"

Something about that scent was driving Josie mad. It was a smell connected to her memories, the ones that wouldn't quite come to her. A door, a tunnel, and that scent. And a word…a single word that held a lot of weight. It had almost registered when she was in the library, and now it floated up again in her mind, mysterious and shapeless. If she could just find the edges…

"VILLOU!" she shouted, elated.

Her triumph lasted only for a moment, because as soon as the word left her lips, she and Emily were transported to a strange and terrifying world…right in the middle of an ongoing battle.

Chapter Sixteen
The War

Shadow tore through the castle with guards in tow, ripping paintings off the walls and upending bookcases. A trail of detritus lay in his wake, looking for all the world like a tornado had just spun down the halls.

"M'lord, if you could just tell us why you think the mirror is here…" Rowan began, trying his best to keep up with Shadow.

"Because it's nowhere else!" Shadow screamed, throwing a vase full of flowers to the floor. "I have the entire In Between looking for it, I've threatened them with torture in The Pits if they don't bring it to me, and still nothing! If it's not out there and it's not in here, that means one of my guards must have found it in the rubble and kept it for himself. Is that what you're telling me, Rowan?"

Here Shadow suddenly stopped and turned on his heel, fixing Rowan with a steely look strong enough to wither a rose. Rowan took a large step backward and looked down at the stone floor.

"No sir, I would never say that. I just think…"

"Are you happy with your job, Rowan?"

Rowan faltered. "Sir?"

"Do you want to continue down the path you're on as the highest ranking security officer to the ruler of this land?"

"Sir, of course, I…"

"Then stop thinking. I don't want to hear what you think. Unless you know where I can find that mirror, keep your mouth shut and make yourself useful. I should think you would be happy to do anything I say after the debacle down in the tunnels."

Rowan nodded. "Yes, sir."

"M'lord! Come quickly!"

It was one of the guards who patrolled the outer perimeter of the castle, with a look of alarm on his face that turned Rowan's stomach sour.

Shadow scowled. "What is it?"

"The villagers, sir. They've gone mad."

∞

Andy and Alek stood shoulder-to-shoulder with their friends, lined up across the hill. In the distance, Shadow's castle loomed like a bad omen, a smudge that was barely visible through the smoke and dust that had been kicked up.

A hundred feet away, Kyra and her group stood armed with all the weapons they could find: sharpened sticks, heavy iron pans, and crude torches made of maple wood soaked in kerosene were the most popular. The air felt greasy; Andy followed Alek's lead and pulled his shirt up over the lower half of his face to block some of the fumes.

"It doesn't have to be this way," Alek yelled to the group facing his. "You're only going to put these people in danger!"

"We're willing to face the consequences," Kyra yelled back. She had tied a handkerchief around her nose and mouth, which muffled her words, but her eyes were dark and fierce above it. "We won't live in fear anymore! The World is waiting for us, and we're ready to face whatever is in it rather than stay here and live a half-life."

The group behind her shouted in agreement, waving their torches around wildly. Andy felt his stomach do a slow roll. There would be violence here today, and though their numbers were split almost evenly, he didn't like to think about the odds of success. His group had their own weapons —clubs and gardening tools, mostly—but he wasn't ready to use one of his own against someone, no matter how bad things got. He curled his fists at his side and took a deep, ragged breath.

"We don't want to fight today," he called. "You can stop this now, before it's too late, and work with us to come to a decision. We don't want to stay here, either, Kyra. We just want to have a better plan than storming the castle."

"It's already too late," Kyra spat. "Do you think things will be any easier if we keep putting it off? How many more days or months or years are we going to waste here?"

"How are you going to feel when your friends are dead at Shadow's hands?" Andy countered.

Kyra shook her head. "We're already dead."

And with a great war cry, Kyra lifted the torch high above her head and charged. The group behind her followed, weapons raised, screams rending the air.

∞

Josie and Emily fell into the In Between roughly, landing on a hillside with cries of shock and pain. Emily dropped to one knee with the impact, catching herself on both hands before gravity could pull her down any further. Josie fell on her bottom, sliding down the sloped ground for a moment before coming to a stop. All around them, screams tore into the crimson air.

"Josie?!" Emily said in a panic. "Where are we?"

Josie sat up and looked around, feeling dazed. Just a moment ago they had been in the Bruiser's garage, she recalled, and that magic word had appeared in her mind finally, like a puzzle piece.

"I don't know," she said, getting slowly to her feet. "But it feels familiar."

Emily walked forward hesitantly, surveying the land. In the distance, smoke curled against a darkening sky. "Yeah. It does."

The sisters stood still for a moment, listening. Battle cries were carried on the wind to them from over the hill; far on the horizon, a castle loomed against the stars. Josie and Emily climbed the hill and, standing at the crest, looked down into the valley below.

A battle was raging between two groups. The girls couldn't make out faces from so far away, but nothing about the scene seemed familiar. They watched as a small figure tore through the field with a weapon raised, fighting off anyone who came close.

"I want to get closer," Josie said, never taking her eyes off the figure. Something was pulling at her, tugging at her memory.

"I think that's a really bad idea," Emily said.

"Come on, we can go around and use the treeline for cover. Follow me."

Josie grabbed her sister's hand and ran toward the edge of the woods, moving quickly and surely down the slope with the trees acting as camouflage. She felt that she had been here many times before, so the geography wasn't a challenge; she was able to keep them well hidden as they went. Not that anyone involved in the battle would have noticed; the closer they got, the more detail the girls could see. The fight had obviously been going on for a while. Several wounded figures lay in the dirt, while those who were still standing limped and pulled themselves along. Some used torches to fend off their enemies; others wielded heavy sticks like swords, fencing with them. A fire raged over the next hill, illuminating the gathering purple sky.

"I know this place," Emily said when they stopped running.

Josie pulled her little sister closer to shield her from view. "I feel like I do, too, but I don't know why."

She peered through the trees at the figures in the valley; they were much closer than before, and she could make out faces. A tow-headed boy limped to the side of the battlefield and collapsed, his face blackened with soot; a girl about Josie's age whooped and hollered as she ran at full-speed towards a tall boy with a mess of dark hair. A boy who looked a lot like…

"Andy!" Josie screamed

Emily snapped her head around toward the battlefield and drew in a tight breath. It was Andy alright, unchanged from the pictures she'd seen in their old house.

Fear coiled around her spine. There was something gnawing at her, something important about where they were, but she had no time to think about it.

As time did a slow roll, Emily blinked, and she, Josie, and Andy found themselves transported back to The World.

Chapter Seventeen
Home Again

Is there anything as sinister as a quiet suburban street at night? A picture of peace, lit only with subtle orange sodium lights which draw moths in the summer and become soft halos in winter; it is a place painted with the safety of home and of familiarity. Yet in the velvety shadows just beyond the well-worn sidewalks—some of which still bear the marks of a little girl's abandoned hopscotch game—there sometimes sits a formless and savage threat, eager to devour the next unsuspecting person to come along, and that is what makes the suburban street so terrifying, for it is when we don't suspect evil that it inevitably shows its hungry and skeletal face.

Unfortunately for the girls, their threat followed them right through a rip in the very fabric of time and space, spilling into the twilight of Wicker Way with battle cries still rending the air.

"Josie?"

She turned to find Andy beside her in the middle of the street, pale and in shock, trying to come to terms with what he was seeing.

"Is it really you?" she whispered.

"I think I could ask you the same thing," he said. Tears spilled down his cheeks, cutting clean lines through the dirt and soot.

"I hate to interrupt your reunion, but we need to move," Emily said, pointing down the street. Kyra, Tomas, and the rest of the In Between battle crew were running towards them with weapons still raised, seemingly unaware of where they were. Screams and war cries could still be heard, although Emily had no idea if they were coming from this world or echoing from the other one.

The siblings took off with Andy clutching his wounded side. Kyra had bruised him good with her fist, had maybe even cracked a rib. His mind reeled as they ran through the streets, tiredly comparing the purple skies of the In Between to the dusky twilight of The World. He was having trouble focusing.

As they rounded a corner, Josie spotted a figure riding toward them on a bike. *Great,* she thought. The last thing they needed was to have to explain what was happening. She wasn't even sure she could come up with a reasonable lie, but as the figure pedaled closer, she felt her heart lighten.

"Shanti! Stop!" Josie called, skidding to a halt in front of her classmate.

"What's going on?" Shanti asked calmly. She stilled her bike and slid off in one smooth motion, looking at each of the siblings in turn. If what she saw alarmed her, she never gave any indication.

"There's something big happening back that way, with weapons. Come with us, we're going to find a safe place," Josie panted.

Shanti put down the kickstand with the side of her foot, parking the bike on the side of the road. "Shouldn't we call the police?"

"No time," Josie said, grabbing Shanti's hand. "Come on!"

The group headed south, towards Main Street. Josie didn't have a plan fully formed in her mind but instead let her instincts guide her once more.

"Look, the library!" Josie shouted. The building stood like a beacon, a shimmer in the darkening air. "We'll be safe there!"

Andy and Emily followed, not questioning their sister's logic; it felt right to them, too. They hurried up the walk and to the doors, where a woman with an anxious expression stood waiting.

"Mary?" Josie said.

"Quick, get inside!" the librarian said, pulling them through the double doors before locking them.

"What's going on?" Emily cried as they were ushered through the empty lobby. Mary led them to the back of the library, turning off lights as they went. When they reached the children's section, she motioned for them to sit at a table with her.

"Are you alright?" she asked, studying them carefully.

"We're fine, other than the chaos happening outside," Josie said. "What do you know? Were you waiting for us?"

"I felt the time rip. It shook the entire library. I knew you two were special," Mary said, nodding to Josie and Emily. "Who did you bring through?"

"A big group of people who were fighting," Emily said.

"Fighting?" Mary asked, concerned.

Josie looked at Andy. "I think we got there just in time."

The weight of what had happened fell on her then, and she grabbed Andy and pulled him tightly to her with a sob. They stayed locked together for several moments, crying tears of happiness and frustration and sorrow for all the time they had lost. Emily leaned over and joined them, wrapping her small arms as far as they would go around her brother and sister, and felt herself start to crumble. It had been a long day.

"This is our brother," Josie said finally, pulling away to wipe her eyes. "He's been missing for six years. Someone kidnapped him from his bed in the middle of the night, but we found him in another world. We found him." She choked back a sob on the last word.

"The In Between," Andy said, and both Josie and Emily whipped around to look at him at the sound of the name. "That's what they call it."

"That's right!" Josie said, grabbing Andy's arm in excitement. "I remember now. The tunnels and the trees that looked like cotton candy. And Annika! Is she okay?"

Andy shook his head, attempting to keep the tremor out of his voice and not succeeding. "She was killed the day we escaped. The tunnels collapsed when we went through the portal."

"Oh no," Josie wept, wrapping an arm around her stomach. As memories flooded her brain, she called up the pale, heart-shaped face of the girl who had taken such good care of them when they arrived at the In Between. She had been like an older sister to them both, the girl Josie had been drawing in her sketchbook for years. The news of her death was like a punch in the gut. "She died trying to help us."

"She did. Listen, do you remember the little key we found in the cupboard the first time we traveled to the In Between? It was with a book."

Josie frowned and shook her head. "No, why?"

"Because the Shadow Man is looking for it. I think if I can get it to him, all this will be over."

"The Shadow Man," Josie whispered. "I thought he was just a dream." She turned to look at Andy as a terrifying thought came to her. "Is he looking for you?"

"I don't know. Probably. I'm sure he knows about the time rip by now." Andy swiped at his eyes and smiled at Emily, taking her hand across the table. "You've grown so much. Do you remember me?"

Emily couldn't form words around the lump in her throat; instead, she dissolved into tears and nodded frantically, squeezing her older brother's hand in a gesture of comfort.

Shanti had been watching and listening with great interest, turning her head back and forth between each person in the group like a tennis spectator. "What's a time rip?" she asked now, bringing the siblings back to the present. "What are you guys talking about?"

Mary smiled kindly. "It's hard to explain, but this town has a kind of magical fault line running through it. At its strongest point, it sits right beneath this neighborhood."

"The Bedford Bruiser," Josie said softly. "He lives just down the road from here. On the night my brother disappeared, a giant mirror fell at the Bruiser's house and he was hurt. No one could ever figure out what caused it to fall."

"I see you've been doing your reading!" Mary said approvingly. "There are several spots around Bedford that act as portals to other dimensions; that house is one of them. The library, on the other hand, was built as a safe place for anyone who finds themselves lost. Time and space are different here. Sensitive people—like you, Josie—can feel that difference, can sometimes even find ways to use the fault line to their advantage. Not everyone who figures out how to use that power wants to use it for good, though. Whoever came through on that day caused a powerful rip. I'm sure that's why the mirror fell."

"Magic," Shanti repeated. "Real, actual magic."

"I know it sounds crazy, believe me," Mary said. "I've been a Guardian here for a hundred years, and I still have a hard time reconciling it."

"It doesn't sound so crazy," Shanti said, looking thoughtful. "Our ancestors believed in all kinds of things that seem strange today. Maybe they knew more than we do about the world."

"You're over a hundred years old?" Andy asked Mary incredulously.

"More like two hundred," she replied with a grin. "I just didn't take the job until later in life."

"So that's why Emily and I were able to travel to the other world from the Bruiser's house," Josie said suddenly. "Because it's a portal. But how did we get back here, with a huge group of people who were trying to kill each other?"

"I'm not sure," Mary said. "Unfortunately there are still many things about the other dimensions that we just don't understand yet. One of the few constants is that the massive changes to a person's mind and body when they enter a portal can be extremely unstable. I'm guessing that the people who came through the time rip aren't feeling much like themselves. Once you've lived in one dimension for a long time, it's hard to suddenly be thrust into The World. All the fear and hatred and anger they felt when they were fighting over there is magnified here. It must be chaos outside these doors right now."

The group fell silent for a few beats; in it, they could hear distant sirens.

"I think we need to get back to the house," Emily said finally. "I know this is a safe place, but the aunts are there, and we need to get in touch with Mom."

"I think you're right," Josie said. "Mary, do you have a car?"

She shook her head. "I'm sorry, I walk to work. I can go with you, although I can't guarantee my ability to keep you safe outside of the library, not with the time rip still open. Things are too unstable."

"No, you should stay here in case other people need help," Josie said, pushing back her chair to stand. "We'll go and get back here as soon as we can."

"Jo?"

She looked down at Andy, who was slumped over the table. Dark circles formed half-moons beneath both eyes, and he had broken out in a cold sweat. His lips were so pale they were almost translucent.

"I don't feel so good," he said, and fainted.

Chapter Eighteen
Changes

"Andy?" Josie cried, shaking her brother by the shoulder. Turning to the others, she pleaded, "Help me get him up. I'll carry him on my back."

Mary rushed around the table to assist Shanti in lifting the boy, who was taking slow, shallow breaths. "He may start to come around once you get outside the library. The closer he is to the time rip, the better he'll feel."

"But what if the rip has closed?" Emily asked. The enormity of what Mary was saying floated in the back of her mind, but she couldn't face it just yet.

"No time," Josie said grimly, pulling Andy onto her piggy-back style. "Let's go. Shanti, you should stay here where it's safe."

"Not going to happen," Shanti said. "You won't be able to protect yourself out there while you're carrying him."

The girls looked at one another for a long moment, and Josie could see much in Shanti's eyes.

She recalled the girl's first day in class and how she had seemed so self-assured and confident, so unlike everyone else their age. She had been suddenly thrust into an unbelievable situation with people she barely knew, yet she had remained calm and kind. Whatever happened in the next few hours, Josie was incredibly grateful to have Shanti by her side.

"Alright," she said. "You ready to run?"

∞

Andy began to flicker in and out of consciousness as they ran, feeling a glassy pain in his side now and then as he shifted on his sister's back. Things were murky, almost as if they were underwater. He was vaguely aware of a storm rolling in; thunder punctuated Josie's ragged breathing as she carried him through the darkened streets. Distantly, he could hear the wail of sirens mingling with raised voices. They seemed to be coming from everywhere at once, on all sides. He wanted to tell Josie to be careful, to ask where Emily was, but his strength felt like water swirling around a drain.

Between bouts of darkness, Andy saw strange sights. With his head resting on Josie's shoulder, he watched a group of kids sword-fighting in the middle of the street, saw clouds of smoke floating from the trees, spotted a familiar boy standing agog beside a parked car. The boy's mouth hung open in awe as he ran a hand over the vehicle's hood. Andy wanted to call out to the boy but couldn't remember his name. He had something so important to tell him about the mirror, but things were slipping away more quickly now.

When he opened his eyes again, the house on Wicker Way loomed before them, lit up in the night to welcome them home.

∞

Josie climbed the front steps as quickly as she could, legs trembling with exhaustion. Shanti and Emily were already ahead of her, opening the door so she and Andy could get inside safely. In the foyer, Josie slid Andy off her back as gently as she could and laid him on the floor, where he moaned and shook his head as though he was in the throes of a bad dream.

"Aunt Joan! Aunt Alice!" Josie yelled. "Mom?"

"In the kitchen, dear," Joan called. The rich scent of cookies wafted through the air.

Josie left Emily and Shanti with Andy and ran down the hall, hoping against hope that her mother was home from work. But the kitchen only held her aunts, who looked up in startled concern as Josie appeared in the doorway looking battle-worn and disheveled.

"Good heavens, child, what's happened?" Joan asked, hurrying to Josie's side.

"It's hard to explain," Josie said, bending over with her hands on her thighs to catch her breath. "Just come with me."

In the foyer, Emily sat beside Andy like a nurse, keeping one hand on his shoulder to make sure he was still breathing. She had procured a blanket from somewhere and had draped it over him.

"My god," Alice whispered, moving to Andy's side. "Andrew?"

"Yes," Emily said. Her face was red and splotchy from crying. "And I think he's dying."

"How did this happen? Where did he come from?" Joan cried, kneeling to place a hand on Andy's forehead.

"It's a long story. Can you help me get him into the living room?"

They moved as a group, with Josie and Emily cradling Andy's head while Joan and Alice held his legs. Shanti ran ahead and pushed pillows off the couch to make room for him to lie down.

"Let's take a look," Joan said. Josie was immeasurably grateful to have an adult in the room who could take over for a minute while she caught her breath and gathered her thoughts. "Alice dear, run into the kitchen and get the first aid kit and a warm washcloth."

Josie watched Alice scurry from the room. "She remembered Andy."

"She's been feeling much better the past few days," Joan said, feeling for the boy's pulse. She pulled the blanket away and began to inspect him gingerly, looking for injuries. "I suspect having you girls here has helped her memory quite a bit."

"Where's Mom?" Emily asked. She had moved beside the window and was peering out through the side of the curtain, keeping an eye on the street. Sirens could still be heard keening through the neighborhood, but the house was safe for the moment. Shanti sat on the fireplace hearth, watching patiently.

"Still at work," Joan replied, taking the washcloth Alice had handed her and cleaning off Andy's face with it. "Tell me what happened."

"I'm not sure you'll believe us," Josie said. She was thinking specifically of what they had just been through to get to the house. Running through the streets while trying to avoid various fights and people running wild—some foreign, some not— had been troubling in more ways than one. Not only was the other world spilling into this one, it was already affecting the others who lived here. Fires had spread from block to block, some set in cars or trash cans, others on the lawns of certain homes. Josie recalled what Mary had said about all the anger and rage that had grown during the battle and how it would only blossom here.

"You've shown up looking like you've been through a battlefield, bearing your wounded, long-missing brother. I think I'm inclined to believe whatever you say," Joan said, not unkindly.

Josie nodded. "I don't understand much of it myself, but the gist of it is, Andy was kidnapped by someone and taken to live in another dimension. He's been trapped there for the last six years, but Emily and I found him and brought him back. Now that he's here, away from that other world, his body isn't doing so well."

"How did you get to him?" Joan asked. She had pulled Andy's shirt up and was using her fingertips to feel along his ribcage, looking for broken bones.

"I don't know for sure. I started remembering things from a long time ago, things from the summer, Andy disappeared, and when I spoke a certain word we were transported to the land where Andy was being held. Aunt Joan, this town is a powerful place. There are portals and pockets of magic everywhere."

"Mhmm. Alice, hand me that first aid kit, will you?"

"Joan, are you listening? We have to get my mom home right now."

Josie and Emily exchanged a worried look. Their aunt didn't seem to be taking them seriously despite the sudden appearance of Andy and his troubling condition. Alice had backed slowly across the room until she was standing in the doorway, where she watched events unfold without speaking. Josie didn't know if she was in shock or if she wasn't as well as Joan claimed she was, but whatever the reason, it was unsettling.

"I don't think there's any need for that," Joan said. Josie watched as her aunt pulled a broken hand mirror from Andy's pocket and held it up to the light. Several shards of glass had splintered from it and lodged in his side, and before Josie could move closer to her brother, Joan whispered under her breath, and the slivers of glass pulled themselves free from Andy's skin, flying through the air toward the mirror. There, they reassembled themselves to create a smooth, shimmering surface.

"Emily, back up," Shanti said, moving toward the girl to pull her away from Joan.

The sisters watched as the woman they had known as their aunt began to ripple and change, shedding her skin like a snake. Her gray hair fell from its tidy topknot and slid to her shoulders in a dark sheath. When she looked up at Josie, her kind eyes were gone, replaced with chips of ice that seemed almost to glow in the dim living room.

"Hello, Despoine," the Shadow Man said from the doorway.

He stepped over the threshold and into the room, surveying the scene. Upon seeing his face, the full force of Josie's memories came slamming into her, and she staggered back against Shanti, who held her steady and took her hand, squeezing it to let her know she wasn't alone. Josie reached for Emily with her other hand and shielded her from view.

"Revel," said the woman who had been Josie's aunt. She was someone else entirely now, a new being who radiated power. Josie could feel it vibrating in her fingertips, a kind of electrical pulse that made her feel dizzy.

"Fancy meeting you here," said Shadow. He moved to the far side of the room, where there would be no doorways at his back. "Is this where you've been hiding?"

"Not that I owe you any explanations, but yes," Despoine said coolly, stretching her arms above her head. "It feels good to be back in my own body."

"What made you choose this place?"

"Don't you feel it? This town is a hotbed of magic. I wanted to make sure I wouldn't be easily detected, and that I could travel when I needed to. Bedford was the perfect place."

"Where is my aunt?" Josie asked boldly.

"Where is my mirror?" Shadow countered, stepping forward.

"*Your* mirror?" Despoine laughed. "It was never yours."

"What do you know about it, witch?"

Despoine held up the hand mirror she had taken from Andy's pocket, turning it gently in the light so that it gleamed. "Oh, I know everything about it. It's always been mine."

Shadow faltered. "The night you took Penelope… I saw a flash before you disappeared. You used the mirror to get away."

"Yes, and she stole it from me and hid it somewhere before I wiped her memories clean."

Despoine stood from the couch and walked deliberately toward Shadow, measuring her steps. Her voice was smooth, like a snake in the grass. "I brought Penelope here rather than subject her to our father's wrath. I know you're upset, but why don't we let bygones be bygones? I have the mirror back now, and I can travel anywhere I want. You'll never have to see me again."

Shadow curled his lip in disgust. "And what about the things you took from me? The things your father took from me? Trapped in that hell for years without the woman I love, wondering whether she remembered me or if she was even alive. And you say you took her memories from her? 'Wiped them clean'? *How dare you.*"

"I did what I had to do," Despoine spat. "My father had me under his thumb from the day I was born, always threatening to banish me from Atlantis, *from my home,* if I didn't do as he said. Do you have any idea how terrifying that is for a young girl?"

"You weren't a girl. You were a goddess. You could have used your power for something good, but instead, you systematically destroyed your sister's life, all because you were jealous. And now," Shadow said, moving dangerously close to Despoine, "you are going to tell me where she is."

"She's right behind you," said Despoine.

Alice, who had been hiding in the shadows of the hallway, stepped forward timidly.

Chapter Nineteen
Denouement

"Are you following any of this?" Shanti asked Josie in a whisper.

"Some," Josie replied. She was mentally and physically exhausted and trying to keep up with the thread of the conversation was overwhelming. Things were starting to become more and more dreamlike, blurring around the edges. It occurred to her that she was feeling the effects of traveling, but she wasn't sure what to do about it. Fear had been replaced by worry for her brother, who was still lying bloodied on the couch, and her sister, who was trembling behind her.

"What did you say?" Shadow whispered to Despoine. His eyes darkened, twin pools of black that held silver stars deep down inside. He stepped closer to her, enchanting her with every bit of energy he had.

"I had to wipe Penelope's memories so she wouldn't try to find you." Despoine spoke like a person who had been hypnotized. "After we left Mykonos, she tried to escape a few times, and I knew it was only a matter of time before our father found her. What better way to keep someone in the dark about their own identity than by turning them into an old woman with a memory problem?"

Josie looked at Alice, who had inched forward into the room and was looking at Shadow curiously. His shoulders drooped as the tension left his body, and Josie could almost feel the sense of hope he harbored.

"You seem so familiar," Alice said with a little smile.

"Is it really you?" Shadow asked, his voice shivering.

Despoine, finding herself freed from Shadow's enchantment through distraction, saw her opportunity. A sudden, blinding flash burst through the room, pushing Josie and Shanti backward as they turned away from the light. When they were able to open their eyes, Despoine was gone.

"No!" Revel screamed. "She took the mirror!"

Shanti pointed at the air over Alice's head, which had become a shimmering oil slick of pinks and blues. "Look!"

As the room watched, the colors began to slip down over the elderly woman's hair, dripping like paint through the strands and onto her shoulders. Each part the colors touched became something different, twisting into a new form until her entire body was covered. After a moment, she was transformed into a beautiful woman with long, dark hair. Josie watched as she stepped toward Shadow, beaming.

"Revel," she said softly. "You found me."

Shadow fell to his knees, weeping openly. "Penelope," he cried.

She knelt and put her arms around him tightly, shedding tears of her own. "Please don't cry."

Shadow, who had lived for so long in darkness, began to make a transformation of his own. Skin that hadn't seen the World's sun in centuries regained its color, flushing his cheekbones; hair as black as a swatch of velvet began to lighten, curling around his forehead and ears. Josie watched in amazement as the terrifying being she remembered from six years ago was changed into a man who had found his other half.

"I don't understand," Revel said, standing and cradling Penelope's face with both hands. "How did this happen?"

"Despoine cast a spell to keep me in human form. Now that she's gone, her power over me is broken," Penelope said simply.

"And you remember who I am?" Penelope smiled. "I could never forget you, my love."

Andy, who had managed to pull himself up into a sitting position, slumped down once more. His eyes were sunken, and the hollows of his cheeks gave him the appearance of an old man. Josie cried out and ran to his side, taking his hand.

"Andy! Wake up!" She looked up at Revel and Penelope in a panic. "Help him, please!"

Penelope moved to the couch, kneeling beside Josie. "He's been gone for a long time. Being here is destroying his body."

"You have to help him, please," Josie sobbed, running her hand through Andy's hair. She thought of her mother, who would have to mourn her son twice. "We just got him back."

Penelope touched Andy's forehead, ran her fingers down his cheeks and over his eyes. She began to hum as she did so, closing her own eyes. Up and down his arms she went, up and down his legs, around his torso. Josie could feel warmth radiating from the woman's fingertips and remembered what Shadow had said to Despoine: that she was a goddess, which meant Penelope was, too.

The entire room watched as Andy's breathing and color returned to normal, slowly but surely. His face filled out until he had a healthy glow; it was the best Josie had seen him look since she and Emily had found him.

After a moment, Andy opened his eyes and looked around with a weak smile. "I was dreaming of the beach."

Penelope laughed; Josie and Shanti followed suit through tears. Revel stood back, marveling at the woman he loved.

"Thank you, thank you," Josie whispered to Penelope, taking her hand in gratitude. "You have no idea what you've done."

Penelope held onto Josie's hand for a moment and looked into her eyes, a kind smile on her lips. "It was you who found the mirror. You discovered my hiding place."

Josie nodded. "Andy and I found the little door in the basement. I remember the mirror, and a lamp, and a little book filled with writing. It had instructions inside on how to use the mirror to travel."

Penelope looked up at Revel. "That's Despoine's journal. It might be useful if we want to find her."

"It's probably still in the basement," Josie said. "I don't think anyone has gone down there in a long time."

"Yes, I believe you're right. I put an enchantment on the basement when I hid the mirror so that Despoine wouldn't notice it. I was planning to sneak downstairs and escape later that night, but she took my memories and glamored me into Alice's body before I could get back to it. Everything was right beneath her nose the entire time she was here."

"What did she do with my aunts?" Josie asked, unsure if she really wanted to know.

Penelope shook her head. "I'm not sure, but I don't have much hope that they are still alive. I'm so sorry, Josie."

"Where did Despoine go?" Andy asked.

"We don't know, and that's a problem," Revel said. "I have no way to travel without the mirror, and after seeing what happened to the boy, I don't want us to stay here too long."

"Can't you use the time rip to go back to the In Between?" Josie asked.

He shook his head. "I never want to go back there. It's not home. Penelope and I need to find a place of our own. I won't take a chance on going back and getting trapped again."

"You won't be trapped," Emily said.

Everyone turned to look at the youngest Burns sibling, who was still quietly standing in front of the window.

"What do you mean?" Revel asked.

Emily sat down on the arm of the couch. "I've been feeling weird since we moved here; my memories are all mixed up, and I've been having trouble sleeping. Earlier tonight, when we were at the library, I realized that it didn't just start when we moved to Bedford. It's been going on for years. Seeing Andy again made me remember. "

Josie knelt beside her sister and look up in concern. "What are you talking about, Em?"

"I started sleepwalking when I was little," Emily said. "I would wake up and find myself in the kitchen in the middle of the night, or in the back-yard—"

"You never told me that!" Josie cried.

"Because I didn't understand it. It scared me at first, but the more it happened, the more I got used to it. I never knew where I would end up, though. Once, I woke up in your closet."

Josie remembered the night before the move when she had woken up from a dream about Andy and heard clothes hangers clanging together in the closet.

"And then one night," Emily continued, "I woke up in a different place. A park, next to a pond, with stone fountains all around. I walked for a little while in the dark until I came to a street, and when I looked up, I saw the Eiffel Tower."

"You're a traveler, just like the Shadow Man," Andy said softly.

Emily nodded. "I don't know how or why, but yes. I got so scared that night, I panicked, and a few seconds later I was standing in the hallway of our house. I couldn't control it."

"My god," Josie said.

"I was there, in the In Between, when you and Andy were caught in the tunnels. I overheard you guys talking about what you'd found in the basement, and I wanted to be included, but I knew you'd never let me go with you. So I followed you through the portal. I wasn't old enough then to read the instructions on how to travel, but I didn't need them, and I didn't need the mirror."

"You gave Annika the river water, down in the tunnel," Andy said. "I thought it was Alek in all the confusion, but it was you."

"I don't remember doing that," Emily said. "In fact, I don't remember a lot about my time there, or anywhere else I traveled. Going back there today—and then coming through the time rip—opened up some memories, but there are still a lot of holes."

She turned to Revel and Penelope, who had been listening intently. "I don't know why I have this power or where it came from, but I don't want it. Will you take it?"

Revel took Emily's hand and knelt before her. "I've never met anyone like me. Another who could travel, I mean. That's a very special gift you have, young lady. Are you sure you don't want to keep it?"

"I'm sure," said Emily. "I can't control it, and fear seems to be the only way I can get back to where I came from. I don't want to live that way, being scared all the time. I don't need it. But you do."

Revel looked closely at her. "Emily. What's your full name, dear?"

"Emily Marie Burns. Why?"

"E. M. Burns," Revel said, shaking his head with a chuckle. "I thought I was looking for a key that would open a door, but all this time, it was a little girl."

Emily looked around. "Does anyone know what he's talking about?"

Revel smiled. "It doesn't matter. I will be very happy to take your traveling powers, Miss Emily. I think Penelope can help us with that."

"Indeed I can," Penelope said. "Are you ready to meet your son?"

"My son," Revel said. "Where is he?"

"Mykonos, a demi-god well-hidden amongst the other islanders. It was the last thing I was able to do before Despoine brought me here. He grew into a strong, beautiful man, just like his father. I cannot wait for you to meet him."

Penelope turned to Emily. "Are you ready, child?"

"I think so," Emily said, taking a deep breath.

Andy pulled himself into a sitting position once more, taking Josie's hand. She felt Shanti kneel beside her and leaned against her friend's arm, suddenly more tired than she had ever been in her life.

"I am so lost right now," Shanti said. "But I can't wait to hear the whole story from you when this is all over. I'm glad I met you, Josie."

Josie snorted laughter through her tears. "I'm sorry we dragged you into this, Shanti. But I'm so glad we met, too."

They watched in reverent silence as Revel, Penelope, and Emily linked hands; within moments, a golden light began to emerge from Penelope's fingertips and spread downward, enveloping her arms and torso. The illumination was so bright that Josie turned away, covering her eyes; a faint humming sound filled the room briefly and then was gone.

"Is it done?" Emily asked. "I don't feel any different."

"That might have something to do with the time rip," Revel said. "We'll handle that on our way out."

"I'll go downstairs and get the journal," Josie said.

"Will you make sure all the people who came through get back safely?" Andy asked Revel. He was thinking of Tomas and Alek.

"Of course," Penelope said with a smile. "I think a little enchantment is due for the people in this neighborhood. They have lots to forget."

"I have much to atone for, I think," said Revel. "Being trapped in that place for so long, not knowing what had happened to my wife and child…it changed me, and not for the better. I'm not proud of the things I did over there, and I don't know if I can ever make up for them. But I will set things right for all those who were kept in the In Between, and you have my word on that."

Revel held out a hand to Andy, who shook weakly.

"For what it's worth, I'm sorry for everything," Revel said.

"Thank you," said Andy, and he meant it. "Good luck."

Josie, Shanti, Emily, and Andy watched as Revel and Penelope walked out the front door and into the night, a traveler and his goddess on their way to a new life.

"I'm so tired," Emily said.

"I feel like I haven't slept in days," said Josie, stretching out on the floor. "I can't believe Despoine got away. I hope Penelope finds her and makes her pay for what she did."

"I'm sorry about your aunts," Shanti said, "But I believe in karma, and I think Despoine has a big dose of it coming her way."

The four of them sat quietly for a little while, processing everything that had happened, and slowly they all felt the effects of the time rip wearing off. Andy wished he could have seen Alek and Tomas one more time, but it was better that they were on their way home without a sad goodbye. They had been through a lot.

Emily got up and looked out the window. "The fires are out, and I don't hear any more sirens. Penelope and Shadow must have kept their word. One of us should go to the library and let Mary know we're okay."

"I should probably get home," Shanti said. "I wonder if my bike is still parked where I left it?"

"Hopefully it wasn't a casualty of war," Josie said, "But if it was, I'll buy you a new one."

"What are we going to tell Mom about all this?" Emily asked, plopping on the couch beside Andy.

"I don't know, but I'd like to suggest we move someplace far, far away from Bedford," Josie replied.

"That," Shanti said, smiling at her friend," Would be a very sad thing."

The sound of a car pulling into the driveway startled them all, and Josie jumped up to run to the door. She made it to the hall right as her mom came in.

"Hey, Jo," Elizabeth said, dropping her keys on the table in the foyer. "Are you feeling alright? Your cheeks are flushed."

"Mom, I have to talk to you—"

"Where's your sister? Have you both done your homework?"

"It's really important and I think you should—"

"Josie, I'm tired. Can I sit down first?"

She made her way into the living room just as Andy sat up from the couch with a smile.
"Hi, Mom."

About the Author

Amanda Crum is the author of *The Fireman's Daughter* and *Ghosts of The Imperial*. Her work can be found in publications such as *Barren Magazine*, *Blue Moon Literary and Art Review*, and *Ghost City Review*, as well as in several anthologies. Her first chapbook of horror poetry, *The Madness In Our Marrow*, made the shortlist for a Bram Stoker Award nomination in 2015. She was also a finalist for the 2019 J.F. Powers Prize In Short Fiction for her short story, "A Shimmer In The Parlor." She currently lives in a tiny town in Kentucky.

If you enjoyed this book, please consider leaving an online review. The author would appreciate reading your thoughts.

Visit Amanda's author page at Amazon:
https://www.amazon.com/Amanda-Crum/e/B07P9RG4JD/
ref=dp_byline_cont_pop_ebooks_1

You can also follow Amanda on social media:
Goodreads Author: https://www.goodreads.com/author/show/
2904138.Amanda_Crum
Twitter: https://twitter.com/MandyGCrum
FaceBook: https://www.facebook.com/AmandaCrumAuthor/